Cast in Shadow

Shadow SEALs

USA Today Bestselling Author

Abbie Zanders

Cast in Shadow

First edition. February, 2022.

Copyright © 2022 by Abbie Zanders
All rights reserved.

Written by Abbie Zanders.

Cover Design: Cat Johnson

Cover Image: Eric McKinney, 6:12 Photography

Cover Model: CS

Editor: Jovana Shirley, Unforeseen Editing

ISBN: 9798413201169

No part of this book may be reproduced or transmitted in any form or by any means, electronic or mechanical, including photocopying, recording, or by any information storage and retrieval system without the written permission of the author, except for the use of brief quotations in a book review.

This book is a work of fiction. Names, characters, places, and incidents either are products of the author's imagination or are used fictitiously. Any resemblance to actual persons, living or dead, events, or locales is entirely coincidental.

Acknowledgements

Special thanks go to members of my readers group, the Zanders Clan for all of their love, help and constant support. In particular:

- My reader group, the Zanders Clan for making sure I answered ALL the questions.
- My amazing ARC Angels team, who help ensure that what you're reading is as close to error-free as it can get, and for providing such great snippets and quotes for teasers and promo.

And thank YOU. You didn't have to pick up this book, but you did.

CHAPTER ONE

~ *Zeke* ~

"I'M LOOKING FOR RAGUEL."

Without lifting his head, Zeke Ericsson glanced up from the intricate backpiece he was inking at the mention of the name. The brief glimpse was enough to take a mental snapshot he could study at his leisure.

Zeke returned his gaze to the skin under his machine. The young woman who'd spoken was barely out of her teens, if that. Her clothes were fashionably appropriate, but too new and nice for this section of town. The shoes alone were enough to get her jacked. She wasn't the type who typically came into Snake's shop, looking for ink late at night, but she was trying to make it appear as if she was. And if she was asking for Raguel, she had come seeking something else.

Exactly how she'd known to come to Snake's, he didn't know. Zeke sometimes picked up some side jobs—for a fee, of course—and eventually, word got around.

He tuned in to her voice while his hand moved with skill, shading in a talon to make it look as if the dragon's claw was lifting right off the guy's back. Zeke was known for his 3D effects. This one, apparently, was the last one he'd do in this town.

"Sorry, kid," Snake rumbled from the station closer to the front, his voice rough like the engine of the Chopper he rode. "No one here by that name."

Zeke could feel her eyes scanning the room. Knew the moment they landed on him. And stayed there. He pretended to be unaware.

"Well, if he *does* show up, tell him I need to speak with him. It's important. Really important. I'll be at the twenty-four-hour diner down the street. Oh, and I have cash."

She added the last almost as an afterthought, then turned and went back out the way she came, taking the weight of her gaze with her, but he'd gotten the message.

"Crazy bitch," Snake muttered.

She sure was, Zeke thought, if she expected to garner his services. Maybe she was legit. Probably not.

He finished the tat and cleaned the guy up, and then handed him a mirror and led him to the full-length three-way to check out the final product.

"It's fucking awesome, man," the guy said, bumping elbows appreciatively.

Zeke was glad he'd been able to finish the backpiece. It had taken six months and as many sessions, but it had come out beautifully.

He wiped down his station and cleaned his tools, quietly slipping his favorite machines into protective cases and stuffing them into his backpack while Snake flipped the Open sign to Closed.

Snake reached into the till and handed him a wad of bills—his share of the take for the day. Zeke brought a lot of business into the shop, but Snake kept a substantial cut for himself. Zeke didn't care. He'd worked in worse places for less pay, and Snake was a decent enough guy.

"Are you heading to the diner?" Snake asked.

Though they'd never actually spoken about it, Snake had his suspicions about who Raguel was. Snake was a sharp guy and knew a lot about what went on in his town. But Zeke had learned his lessons well, and right there at the top was, *trust no one*. Raguel was a shadowy, unidentifiable figure for a reason.

Zeke paused, turned, and looked Snake right in the eye. "Why would I?"

Snake scratched the back of his neck. He tended to do that when he was anxious. Zeke's gut hummed with warning, just as it always did when something didn't feel right.

"Seems like she's looking for help."

"Unless she's looking for ink, I can't help her. Maybe not even then. She looks like a screamer."

"Yeah, you're probably right." Snake exhaled and dropped the subject. "See you tomorrow."

Doubtful.

When his gut started humming, it was time to get out of Dodge. He'd ignored his instincts once, and the consequences had been devastating. It was yet another life lesson that had been indelibly engraved on his soul—*listen to your instincts*.

Aloud, he said, "Yeah, maybe."

Snake laughed, but that sounded off too. Tense. Worried. Anything that made a big, tough guy like Snake tense or worried didn't bode well.

Zeke avoided the diner, choosing instead to take the scenic route back to the cheap motel, where he'd been parking his ass. His plan: grab his go bag and get the fuck out.

With only a block to go, the hairs on the back of his neck prickled in warning, seconds before two guys stepped out of the shadows.

Zeke recognized the two as enforcers for a local mobster who went by the name of Fat Tony. Fat Tony thought a lot of himself, but it was simply a case of a little bit of power going to a guy's head. He was middle management in the grand scheme of things. He had neither the smarts nor the balls to be anything more. The only reason he was in the position he was, was because he'd married the boss's sister.

Raguel *might* have had something to do with putting one of Fat Tony's guys in the hospital when the guy had been squeezing the local mom-and-pop store a little too hard. Usually, Zeke charged a premium for side jobs, but that one, he'd done pro bono.

"The boss wants to have a word with you," the shorter, stockier thug said.

Your boss, not my boss, you piece of shit. "About what?"

"Doesn't fucking matter, does it?" asked the taller one. "The boss wants to talk, you come and talk."

Zeke weighed his options, then nodded. "Sure. Yeah. I'm not doing anything anyway."

The short guy chuckled. "See? I knew you were a smart guy. Didn't I tell you he was a smart guy, Vin?"

* * *

Less than an hour later, Zeke was back to his original plan: grabbing his shit and ghosting.

No good deed goes unpunished, he murmured to himself. One of these days, he was going to learn his lesson. Still, he couldn't seem to stop himself. He'd always had a soft spot for underdogs.

He passed the diner on the way to the bus station and saw the girl who'd come into Snake's shop earlier, sitting in front of the window, frowning at her phone. In openly seeking Raguel, she'd ensured his departure.

Raguel. The archangel of justice.

Zeke put his head down and continued on. He

was no archangel, but he did have a problem with people who used their power and influence to hurt others. Like Fat Tony and his enforcers, who built their fortunes by extorting honest, hardworking people.

Their mantra: pay or *pay*.

It was the same everywhere. Big cities, small towns, the fucking US government. The rich and powerful wanted to stay that way and would do so by any means necessary, including destroying the lives of good people.

He'd seen it his whole life. First in the trailer park, where he'd spent a good part of his youth, then later in the service as a special ops man. He'd had a front row seat to more than one show. Even gotten to star in a few himself.

These days, he stuck to the shadows. He did his best work behind the scenes. Contract work was always available, and it helped him keep his skills sharp. The government had invested a lot in his training and development. Seemed a damn shame to let it all go to waste.

Zeke made it to the bus station and bought a ticket for the next coach out. The destination was irrelevant. The only thing that mattered was being gone before someone discovered that his meeting with Fat Tony and the boys had ended badly—for them, obviously.

By the time he stepped off the bus ten hours later, he was two states away from where he'd started. He found a dive motel next to a fast-food place, paid cash, and got himself a room.

He took the necessary precautions, which included securing the room and crafting an escape plan. Both had become second nature. After getting a hot shower and wolfing down some food, he turned on the television and allowed himself to relax enough to fall into a deep sleep.

CHAPTER TWO

~ *Aggie* ~

AGGIE PICKED UP THE CASH TIP and slipped it into her pocket with one hand while wiping down the bar with the other. The night had passed without incident, and yet she couldn't shake the sense of foreboding that had been building over the past few hours. Her internal warning system hadn't failed her yet, which meant something was going to happen soon.

She scanned the room again. Still dark. Still smoky. Nothing had changed in the five minutes since she'd last looked. The same guys were still playing pool and shooting darts, though they'd shifted their positions. People hung around the bar and at tables, bitching and moaning about their lives and jobs, drinking beer and eating deep-fried bar food to cope. Rochelle, the young server working the tables tonight, flirted shamelessly with one of the plant guys, laughing and playfully swatting his arm as he tugged her down onto his lap.

That same guy had propositioned Aggie just a

short while before. He met her eyes over the server's shoulder, palmed the young woman's backside, and gave Aggie a wolfish grin, as if to say, *This could have been you.*

Aggie laughed and shook her head. The guy was a notorious flirt, but he was harmless. The female attention he got was freely given and, from the stories Aggie had heard from behind the bar, worth the effort.

The door opened, bringing in a cool rush of night air. Shouted greetings rang out when Sam entered the bar with a couple guys from his second-shift crew. He waved back and headed right to the bar.

"Hey," he said to Aggie with a tired but genuine smile.

"Hey yourself."

Aggie put a circular tray on top of the bar and filled it with drafts. Sam took one for himself and let Rochelle carry the rest to the table where the others had settled. Instead of heading over with them, he hung back at the bar.

Aggie didn't mind. The tavern wasn't busy, and Sam was a nice guy. They'd even gone out a few times, but Aggie had made it clear Parryville was just a temporary stop on her personal journey, and she wasn't interested in anything more than friendship. He seemed okay with that. He'd even told her once that it simplified things, though it was hard to imagine life in Parryville getting much simpler than it already was. People were born here, lived and worked here, had families, and then died here.

"Rough night?" Aggie asked, noticing he looked wearier than usual.

Stress lines pulled at his handsome, if somewhat rugged, face.

He exhaled. "Yeah."

She glanced over at the table. None of the other guys seemed to have anything heavy weighing on their minds.

"Want to talk about it? Bartenders are great listeners, you know, and I'm better than most."

"Yes, you are." He smiled, but it faded quickly. "Can I ask you something?"

"Shoot."

"Do you ever feel like you're in over your head?"

Such a simple question on the surface, but so much unspoken beneath it.

"Sometimes," she answered honestly. "But it's different for me. When things get to be too much, I just move on."

He nodded and lifted the mug to his lips. "Maybe I should take a page out of your book."

"No reason why you can't."

"My whole life is here."

She shrugged. Unlike her, most people had roots or, at the very least, connections that kept them in one place. Walking away from that could be scary, she supposed. She wouldn't know.

"Your life is wherever you make it. Doesn't have to be static."

He thought about that for a moment. Considered the possibilities, then asked, "Would you go with me if I did?"

She crossed her arms and leaned forward on the bar. His eyes dipped to her cleavage.

"Maybe. Depends on when and where."

His eyes rose again to meet hers, and that was when she saw it. A momentary flash of fear. The sense of foreboding she'd been feeling all evening grew stronger.

"Are you in some kind of trouble, Sam?" she asked softly. When he didn't answer right away, she prompted, "Anything I can help with?"

"Yeah. Another beer would be great."

"You got it."

Aggie poured him another draft, then moved to the far side of the bar to take care of the customers down there. Rochelle approached with orders for more rounds, and Sam joined his coworkers and shot a few games of pool. The rest of the evening passed without incident, and Sam said nothing more about what was bothering him. Before long, Aggie was making last call.

"Can I walk you home?" Sam asked.

"Sure. But I'm not going to invite you up when we get there."

He grinned. While their relationship had been

strictly platonic up to this point, Aggie suspected Sam would be amenable to something more if she suggested it.

"One of these days, you're going to change your mind and decide to live on the edge."

She laughed. He had no idea how edgy her life really was. "Maybe. But it won't be tonight."

"Fair enough."

They walked through the quiet streets. A soft breeze blew around them, carrying with it the scents of the nearby river and the chemical smell from the paper plant. Aggie had become accustomed to it over the last couple of months and hardly noticed it anymore.

They didn't talk much. Sam seemed distracted and preoccupied, and Aggie was glad when they arrived at her building.

"Are you sure you're okay?" she asked.

"Yeah, no worries." He reached out and pulled her into a tight hug, then released her just as quickly. "Lock your doors, okay?"

"I always do," she assured him.

"Good night, Aggie."

"Good night, Sam."

That was weird, Aggie thought as she climbed the steps to her second-floor apartment. Sam wasn't an impulse hugger, which confirmed how vexed he was.

She locked the door, just as she'd promised, and moved to the window. She watched Sam's dark silhouette in the glow of the streetlamps, moving at a brisk clip.

Aggie removed her jacket and hung it on the post by the door, then began lighting the soy candles she had placed strategically throughout the room to counterbalance the lingering aromas of stale smoke and mustiness that permeated the old building.

Next, she turned on the soothing white-noise machine and moved to the bathroom, where she started the shower. The ancient plumbing protested with a series of clangs and sputters, but soon, the small room began to fill with steam. Aggie stripped out of her clothes, popped out her contact lenses, and stepped under the hot water to wash away the layers of makeup and the stench of smoke and booze.

She closed her eyes and inhaled the scents of sweet basil and lemon, appreciating their calming and clarifying effects as she scrubbed, exfoliated, and shaved. She followed that up with an indulgent moisturizing cream. The nightly ritual centered her and formed the bridge between who she was and who she appeared to be.

Bartending the closing shift at McTavey's Tavern wasn't her life goal, but it was a great way to get up close and personal with the predominantly blue-collar community, most of whom were employed by the paper plant. The mill illegally dumped toxic waste into the river, and whatever they couldn't flush into the water, they hauled—equally illegally—to a privately owned landfill. Those unlawful activities were what had brought her to Parryville.

Aggie donned a fresh pair of undies and a soft cotton tee, then raided her mini fridge. She selected a container of Greek yogurt, organic granola, and a banana, and then she warmed up some coconut milk and stirred in some ethically sourced vanilla-bean sugar.

The bed creaked under her slight weight as she settled onto it, sitting cross-legged with cheap dollar-store pillows stacked up behind her back. Snacks and water were within easy reach on the side table.

The decor wasn't what she would have chosen for herself, but her current digs were more about projecting the proper image than personal preference. The second-floor apartment had come cheap, furnished, and suitable for a young, single woman traversing the country on a personal journey of self-discovery.

Laptop on thighs, black-rimmed glasses perched on her nose, she fired up the machine, then waited for her custom, secure VPN to do its thing. Once that was up and running, protocols were initiated, connections were established, and files were unlocked.

Now, her *real* job began.

The first thing she did was kick off her

lurkers—the custom searches she'd created to move quietly across the web without detection—targeting financial institutions, real estate agencies, watchdog agencies, and government sites. Her list of keywords and contacts had been steadily growing as she gathered more names. Every day, she added another piece to another puzzle. Who was involved. Who was getting paid. Who was getting paid off. The what, when, where, and how of dirty, greedy businesses.

She sat back and savored her yogurt while the software did its thing. This was her life. A cycle that was repeated over and over again. Another town. Another target. But essentially, her purpose was the same.

Aggie wasn't naive enough to believe she could put an end to corporate greed and government corruption, but she knew she'd never be able to live with herself if she didn't at least *try* to do something. She was a lot like her brother in that respect, though they had chosen vastly different paths to achieve their objectives.

The soft chime from her laptop brought her out of her thoughts and back to the present. A large transfer had just been initiated from one of the shady corporate accounts she was watching. Her fingers flew across the keys, siphoning off the information while simultaneously transposing a few numbers before the funds reached their final destination. That would buy her some time.

She redirected the funds through a scrubber, one that removed any identifying source info. There, the money was divided up into much smaller amounts and transferred in tiny batches to a series of bank accounts she'd opened across the country under a myriad of aliases. To anyone looking at the accounts, the revenue would appear as direct deposits from a legitimate business.

A feeling of immense satisfaction washed over her, knowing that money that would have been spent by some already-too-rich billionaire on something completely superfluous would instead find its way into homeless shelters, animal rescues, and soup kitchens, among other things.

She repeated the process twice more before the pull of sleep became too strong to ignore. When all was said and done, she'd transferred one-point-two million out of the hands of crooks and into the hands of those who needed it most. Not bad for a night's work.

Aggie scrubbed the laptop, erasing all traces of her efforts. She took a few moments to perform a series of relaxing yoga poses, then slipped in between the sheets, followed by a period of mindful breathing to clear her mind before falling into a deep, contented sleep.

It seemed as if only a few minutes had passed before she heard it—the sound of someone breaking into her apartment. Instantly awake, Aggie slipped out of bed and grabbed the pepper spray and Taser she kept within reach, and then she melded quietly into the shadowy recesses of her closet. She quickly pulled on a pair of leggings and shoes.

Whoever they were, they weren't particularly concerned with being sneaky. She clearly heard heavy footfalls on the ancient hardwood, as well as the telltale squeak of the bedroom door opening. The bedroom light came on, slipping beneath the closet door in a narrow strip.

"Where the fuck is she?" said a gruff male voice.

The footsteps grew closer. "She's here somewhere. Check the closet."

Heart hammering, Aggie held her breath and prepared for battle. The closet was small; there was nowhere to hide. If they looked inside, they would see her.

The door opened. Aggie held up the pepper spray and gave the guy a full blast in the face, then sprinted past him as he roared. A second guy placed himself between her and the bedroom door, blocking her exit. She pointed the Taser at him and fired. Two barbed darts shot out, penetrating his clothing and lodging into his skin, creating a circuit that instantly brought him to his knees.

Aggie vaulted over him and bolted through the doorway. The sight of a third man altered her plans. She juked left and headed for the fire escape outside the kitchen window. She yanked hard and threw open the sash, managing to get one foot out onto the rickety contraption before a strong hand wrapped around her ankle and forcibly tried to haul her back inside.

Aggie grabbed at the railing and held on with both hands, kicking out with her free foot. She connected, feeling the satisfying crunch of cartilage beneath her heel. Unfortunately, it didn't stop him. It only pissed him off. He yanked harder, the swift, brutal tug effectively dislocating her ankle.

Aggie howled in pain as her shoulders fought against the same fate. He twisted her foot, and in the resulting agony, Aggie loosened her grip and was hauled roughly back inside, her ribs bumping painfully on the sill and expelling the air from her lungs in the process.

She screamed and scratched and fought, but it was no use. The guy was too big. Too strong.

And apparently, he'd had enough. A fierce, blinding pain at her temple was the last thing she remembered before she lost consciousness.

CHAPTER THREE

~ *Zeke* ~

ZEKE HAD NO PLAN. That was the great thing about drifting—he didn't need one. He had enough cash in his pocket to keep him going for a while, as long as he was smart about it. Eventually, he'd find a place he wanted to stay in for more than a night or two, preferably one with a decent tattoo shop, where he could pick up some work. If that didn't pan out and he needed money, someone was always looking to hire a day laborer.

Several days after his abrupt departure, he was holed up in yet another roadside motel, skimming through cable channels, feeling inexplicably unsettled. Something was coming down the pike; he felt it in his bones, like an approaching storm. Exactly what *it* was, he didn't know, but the feeling had been growing steadily, so he figured it wouldn't be long before he did.

He was drifting in the subspace between restful sleep and semiconsciousness when the sound of his cell phone chime brought him instantly back to full alertness. He carried a burner for emergencies, but he rarely used it, and no one had the number.

And yet ... it was ringing.

He hauled himself out of bed and extracted the phone from his jacket pocket, eyeing the *Unknown* caller ID. It was probably just a robocall, his number just one of thousands some AI bot dialed every hour. Irritated and wide awake once again, he powered down the phone and tossed it on the table on his way to the bathroom to take a piss.

Almost immediately, it started ringing again

Zeke leaned back and looked through the open doorway in disbelief. Had he not held the power button down long enough? A bad feeling churned in his stomach, and it wasn't because of the questionable food he'd ingested.

He finished his business, washed his hands, and turned the phone off again, holding the button down until the screen went black. The device was still in his hand when it came right back on and rang again. Either the phone was defective, or someone had the ability to turn it on remotely. He sure as hell hoped it was the former, because the implications of the latter wasn't something he wanted to consider.

Annoyed, Zeke thumbed the Answer Call icon and held the device to his ear, ready to let loose a string of profanities.

Before he could, however, a silky-smooth woman's voice purred into his ear. "Chief Warrant Officer Ericsson."

Zeke tensed at the address. He wasn't that man anymore. Hadn't been since the day the Navy dishonorably discharged him and told him not to let the door hit his ass on the way out.

"Wrong number." He disconnected the call and tossed the cell onto the bed as if it were going to bite him.

It rang again immediately.

Because of course it did.

Since turning it off didn't seem to have an effect, he considered alternatives. Dropping it in the toilet, for instance, or perhaps crushing it under the heel of his boot.

The ringtone changed. Instead of the standard default, it played the opening chords of a song. One that chilled his bones. *Drift and Die.* The last time he'd heard that particular melody, he and his team had been preparing to walk into what would become his worst nightmare.

He moved to the window and peered out from the side of the drawn blinds, scanning the parking lot below. Rain was visible in the glow of the streetlights, but he saw nothing unusual or suspicious. No cars that hadn't been there before. No dark figures lurking in the shadows.

He crossed the room and looked through the fish-eye peephole in the door. Saw nothing. Heard nothing.

Only that damn phone.

He picked it up and answered for a second

time. The woman laughed softly, a dangerous sound that sent a shiver down his spine.

"I don't make mistakes, Mr. Ericsson."

"Who are you? What do you want?"

"You can call me Charley. Quite simply, I want you."

He pulled the phone away from his ear and stared at it for a full five seconds before bringing it back to his face. "I don't know who the fuck you are, lady, or how you got this number, but I'm not for sale."

Another silky chuckle. "That's not what I've heard, *Raguel*. What did you think of that burger, by the way? I prefer mine without onions, but to each his own."

Zeke clamped his lips together, his brain working overtime. This woman knew his former rank. Knew his moniker. Knew his burner cell number and what he'd had for dinner.

He checked the windows and door again.

"I know all about you, Mr. Ericsson," she continued, as if reading his mind.

"Yeah? What do you think you know?"

"I know you didn't do what the Navy accused you of. I know you have a thing for helping those in need—for a price. I know you live in the shadows, a transient existence, and wish for more. I want to grant your wish."

"What are you, my fairy godmother?"

"Something like that," she said, amusement

coloring her tone.

What the actual fuck? Who is this woman?

He answered his own question. *Not anyone you want to deal with.*

"Sorry, *Charley*. Not interested."

He disconnected the call. Unsurprisingly, it rang again. He didn't answer it. Then, the room phone began to ring. He ignored it, too, and gathered his things, leaving the burner behind. He'd pick up another one on his way out of town.

Except ... the same thing happened at the next town. And the next.

Whoever this Charley was, she was good—he'd give her that. She had eyes and ears everywhere. Knew his every move.

After four days, he was faced with a choice—go completely off-grid or find out what she wanted from him. His curiosity got the better of him.

Zeke settled on the motel bed after dinner and waited. The phone rang within seconds, just as he knew it would.

"All right, I'm listening," he said finally.

"I have a proposition for you, Mr. Ericsson, one I think you will find appealing."

He doubted it. "What proposition?"

"A packet has been left at your door. Review it. I'll be in touch."

This time, she was the one who disconnected.

Zeke went to the door and retrieved the brown packet. He looked up and down the walkway and saw no one. He brought the envelope into his room and considered the wisdom of opening it. What if it contained something deadly or harmful?

He almost laughed at that. If it did, would it be such a loss? It wasn't as if anyone beyond the unlucky fuck who'd be charged with removing his remains would notice or care.

Besides, he rationalized, if this Charley wanted him dead, there were easier, less public ways to make that happen, and she'd already proven repeatedly that she could get to him if she wanted to. A smart man knew when to shut up and listen.

He ripped open the envelope and dumped the contents on the bed. A wallet-sized photo, a wad of cash, and a business card.

The photo was of a young woman. Mid to late twenties. Chestnut-brown hair and big hazel eyes peered out at him from behind thick black frames. She was pretty with petite, fae-like features. He turned the photo over in his hand. No name. No information.

He set it aside, picked up the money, and counted it. Ten thousand in slightly used, mixed denominations.

He put that down, too, and looked at the business card. Matte black with an engraved bird in a metallic hue. No name. No number. Just a handwritten note in neat script, done in metallic Sharpie: *For your time.*

He snorted at that and looked at the photo

again. He couldn't count how many pictures he'd been handed over the years with one order or another. Locate. Recover. Eliminate.

He couldn't help wondering, *Who is she? A target? A package?* He sincerely hoped she wasn't a target. He didn't have a hell of a lot of rules these days, but one he was adamant about was not hurting women or kids.

He peered into the envelope again, thinking there had to be more but there wasn't. No instructions, no directive. What the fuck was he supposed to do with that?

He tucked everything back into the envelope and snorted, not caring much for Charley's methods. They reeked of bureaucracy and government, where the dissemination of information to those carrying out a mission was tightly controlled beneath a premise of *need to know*. Unfortunately, what was *necessary* was subject to interpretation and often grossly underestimated.

He hadn't liked it when he'd been in the Teams. Liked it even less now.

But cash was cash, and if Charley thought a few minutes of his time was worth ten grand, he'd listen to what she had to say before he gave a firm *thanks, but no, thanks* and went on his merry way.

He used some of the money to buy a steak dinner at a nearby roadhouse, then used a little more to pick up a bottle of quality bourbon on the way back to his hotel.

His room was just as he'd left it. The small traps he'd set remained untriggered. No more mysterious, unmarked packages were left at his door. He felt almost disappointed.

Zeke showered and watched lousy television for the rest of the night, biding his time until Charley called again with more info. No doubt, she was giving him time to think and wonder in the hopes of piquing his interest.

He had to admit, he was intrigued. He pulled out the photo of the mysterious female again and studied it, burning the image into his brain, cataloging every feature down to the finest detail. It was her eyes that commanded most of his attention. They were demure. Shuttered. Hinting at great depths and many secrets. Secrets he suddenly wanted to discover.

When Charley called again—*if* she called again—he *might* be inclined to listen.

* * *

There was still no word when he woke the next morning. His latest burner remained silent. Perhaps the situation had changed, and his services were no longer required. A sharp blade sliced across his chest at the thought.

Zeke decided to grab breakfast and coffee. If there was still no word when he got back, he'd simply forget the whole thing and move on. Or at least, he'd try to. He had a feeling those hazel eyes would be haunting him for a while.

Thankfully, another package was waiting for him when he returned. This one contained more cash and a shiny black phone.

He powered on the phone. An eagle appeared, then disappeared in a burst of animated fire. A new image emerged—that of a phoenix rising from the ashes and flying away. The screen went back to black again, and then a static logo faded in—that of an anchor, trident, and phoenix, similar to the Navy SEAL insignia he knew so well.

What message was that supposed to convey? That Charley's organization was made up of a bunch of SEALs who'd been burned, like him? Was this supposed to be a chance for him to rise anew from the ashes?

He laughed at that. If that was what she thought, she'd picked the wrong guy. His past was his past. He'd learned hard lessons and moved on, and he didn't give a shit what anyone else thought. *He* knew the truth, and ultimately, that was all that mattered.

The phone vibrated in his hand, as if she had known the moment he turned it on.

Because of course she had.

"Did you enjoy your pancakes?"

He wasn't as surprised as he'd been the first time. "A little doughy for my taste but edible enough. Are you ready to stop playing games now and tell me what you really want?"

"The woman in the picture. I want you to find her."

He didn't bother asking, *Why me?* He knew why. Because he was damn good at finding people, one of the top SOs—special warfare operators—in the business. He could slip into any situation, any environment, and get the job done.

He might not be a SEAL anymore, but he kept his skills sharp by taking care of scum like Fat Tony and his boys. He provided a service, one that *should* have been performed by cops and lawyers and judges. And he didn't feel bad about taking money for it. They took money to do their jobs. Why shouldn't he?

It wasn't only for the money though. He got a sense of personal satisfaction as well.

The people upon which Raguel meted out justice deserved it. They were criminals, drug lords, and serial abusers with a proven history of fucking people over. Bottom feeders who manipulated the system to their advantage.

Nothing about the woman's picture suggested she met any of his criteria, but looks could be deceiving. Could he find the woman? Absolutely. Would he? That depended.

"Why?" he asked.

Once again, the mysterious Charley seemed to know his thoughts. "I assure you, I mean her no harm. This is for her protection."

He snorted. "I'm going to need more than that."

"I can't offer any more than that until you agree."

"Then, you've made my decision easy. The answer is no."

A moment of silence.

"May I ask why?"

"Because I think you're full of shit. People like you only care about saving your own ass. You don't care about anyone else. If you want her, it's for your benefit, not hers."

Charley didn't miss a beat. "All the more reason why she needs you then, don't you think?"

He laughed, a dark laugh that warned her not to bother trying to stroke a latent protector tendency. He was beyond that. The things he did now, he did because *he* wanted to.

"I already drank that Kool-Aid, and it left me with a bad taste in my mouth. Find someone else."

CHAPTER FOUR

~ *Zeke* ~

DESPITE HIS BEST EFFORTS to forget about Charley and her mysterious offer, the image of the woman in the photo continued to haunt him for the rest of the day and well into the night. He couldn't stop thinking about her. When he closed his eyes, she was there, right behind his lids, silently calling out to him. But what exactly she was saying, he couldn't make out.

Questions hammered him repeatedly on a continuous loop. *Why had she gone missing? Why did someone like Charley care? Was she in danger, and if so, why didn't Charley do something about it?*

She did, jackass. She called you.

The whole situation irked him. And the fact that it irked him irked him even more. He liked his life neat, tidy, mobile, and most importantly, completely under his own control. *He* decided who, when, and if he'd help—no one else. He didn't appreciate Charley's blatant attempts to manipulate him into doing her dirty work.

Therein lay the crux of his problem. This strange pull he felt toward a woman he didn't know was purely a fabrication, crafted by someone who knew a hell of a lot about him, including what buttons to press. Any other explanation was ludicrous. It was impossible to feel more than detached professional curiosity for a woman he'd never met, no matter how far her pretty eyes seemed to reach down into his soul.

Wasn't it?

It didn't matter. He could second-guess himself all day, but the fact was, the more time that passed, the stronger the pull became, and the less inclined he was to sit this one out.

He kept the shiny black phone in sight, waiting for it to ring again, but it remained silent and mocking. Had Charley finally accepted no as an answer and moved on?

He picked up the device and turned it over in his hands. As if sensing his touch, the phoenix logo glowed back into existence. Below it was a hyperlink—*Click Me*.

Zeke's thumb hovered over the text. Was he really going to do this?

Apparently, he was.

He tapped the link, and a list of more hyperlinks appeared.

There were at least two dozen of them, each linking to a different online article from news sites around the country. The dates ranged over a span of about five years.

At first, they seemed completely unrelated. One was about a corporate CEO who lost everything after embezzlement charges were filed against him. Another, about a small, rural mountain town being declared as a superfund site after a high incidence of cancer was reported among the local population. A third detailed the exposure of a human trafficking ring operating under the guise of a women's shelter.

The list went on, each item an example of dirty deeds coming to light through some anonymous do-gooder and justice being publicly served.

Zeke read them all. Then, he read them again. In each and every instance, an unidentified tipster had sent irrefutable proof of wrongdoings into hundreds, sometimes thousands, of inboxes, ensuring they couldn't be ignored. The evidence included names, places, dates, phone records, and in some cases, damning video footage.

That was when Zeke knew why he'd felt a connection to the woman in the photo. Because that haunted, determined look he'd seen in her eyes was the same one he saw in the mirror every morning.

When he closed the last news site, the phone rang with an incoming call.

"All right, you've got my attention."

"She's known as Robin Hood," Charley said without preamble. "In every one of those cases, huge sums of ill-gotten gains disappeared long before the stories hit the news. We have reason to believe she funnels the proceeds to charitable organizations across the country."

"She doesn't keep any for herself?" he asked doubtfully. "How does she fund her philanthropic efforts?"

"She's a skilled hacker," Charley said, sidestepping the question. "Much like you, she's highly transient, and she prefers to remain in the shadows. She stays in low-cost accommodations and seeks out low-wage, under-the-table employment as part of her cover. Once established, she gathers information at the grassroots level, then disappears and finishes the job from elsewhere."

The transience and living under the radar were two more things he could relate to, except when he moved on, he made a clean break and didn't look back.

"Who is Robin Hood really?"

A telling hesitation. "That, I don't know."

Zeke almost snorted aloud. With the power and knowledge Charley had already demonstrated, it seemed unlikely she didn't know Robin Hood's true identity. Yet, his instincts told him two things. One, that Charley really didn't know, and two, that Charley wanted to. When Zeke added one and two, he got three: the order to find and retrieve Robin Hood had come from somewhere *above* Charley, and that was enough to give him pause.

"She's been tracked to several different locations after the fact," Charley continued, "but she uses a different alias each time. She assumes the identity of a real person, someone similar in age and appearance. Temporarily steals their identity, then disappears, resurfacing later in a different location under a different name. Most recently, she's been going by the name of Aggie Mays, and has been working as a bartender in a small town in the northeast."

"If you know that, why do you need me?"

"Because she disappeared several days ago."

"So? You said that's part of her MO."

"Yes, but we have reason to believe this wasn't intentional."

"Why not?"

"Call it an educated guess. A hunch, if you will. You understand hunches, don't you?"

He did, all too well.

Charley wasn't providing full disclosure—he was sure of it. But he was equally as sure that this woman, Robin Hood, *was* in trouble. Exactly what kind remained to be seen. Robin Hood might be running from Charley for all he knew—which could explain his involvement.

"One last question. Why do you care?"

Another telling hesitation. When Charley answered, her voice was quieter. "Because like you, Mr. Ericsson, she performs an invaluable service. We'd like to see it continue."

There was a lot to unpack in that statement, not the least of which was Charley's inference that her organization kept tabs on people like him and the mysterious Robin Hood, and that was some scary shit. He'd never been a fan of Big Brother mentality, and something told him Robin Hood probably wasn't either.

He weighed the pros and cons. There was no doubt he was more intrigued than ever, and it had been a while since he'd faced a real challenge.

Several long moments passed in silence before Zeke said, "All right, I'm in."

"Good," Charley said simply. "You will be provided with everything you need within the hour. There is to be no further contact until she is safely in your custody in a secure location. Time is of the essence. You have two weeks."

"And if it takes longer than two weeks?"

"That would mean I made a grave mistake in hiring you, and as I already explained, I don't make mistakes, Mr. Ericsson."

A soft click signaled the end of the conversation. A familiar sense of anticipation began to flow through his veins as he gathered his things.

CHAPTER FIVE

~ *Zeke* ~

ZEKE TOOK A SEAT AT THE BAR and gave his eyes a chance to adjust to the dark interior. He didn't need clear vision to be aware of the sudden lull in conversations and curious looks being cast his way. He'd expected as much. McTavey's Tavern was a small bar in a small town that catered to locals. Outsiders like him were a curiosity, something to question and be wary of.

It was midafternoon, and the place was pretty dead. No more than half a dozen patrons occupied the space. Among those were three older guys who sat at a scarred square table, their attention temporarily averted from the baseball game playing on a mounted screen in the corner to stare at him.

One of them got up and moved behind the bar. "What can I get you?"

"Whatever you've got on draft is fine."

The guy nodded and poured him a beer with the smooth, rote movements of someone who'd done it thousands of times. Then, he put down a thick cardboard coaster in front of Zeke and set the frosty mug on it.

"Passing through?"

"Looking for someone actually," Zeke said, pulling out his wallet. "I understand she works here."

The bartender's eyes flicked to the photo and flashed with recognition, then looked back at Zeke. Took in his long hair, piercings, and tattoos. Zeke could guess what was going through the guy's mind, and it wasn't, *This guy looks trustworthy. I should tell him everything I know.*

"Sorry. Can't help you."

The guy began to walk away.

Time to change tactics.

The bartender wore a wedding band and looked old enough to have a daughter about Robin Hood's age. The faded American-traditional tattoos on his forearms—an eagle on one and an anchor on the other—suggested he'd done some time in the service.

"She's my sister," Zeke lied easily, casually pushing up his sleeve to display the bone frog ink he hadn't gotten around to covering up yet.

The older man's eyes landed on the tat, just as Zeke had intended. "Your sister, you say?"

Zeke nodded. "You're Mick McTavey, right?"

"I am."

"Aggie told me about this place. Said she liked working here, that the tips were good and you were a decent guy. She's worked in some real shitholes, let me tell you."

Zeke paused and let him digest that for a moment before leaning forward and dropping his voice. "I'm worried about her, Mr. McTavey. She hasn't had an easy time of it, you know? Not since our parents passed. But she's got a stubborn streak a mile wide. She doesn't like to accept help from anyone."

McTavey nodded as if he understood, maybe even had seen evidence of that.

"Like I said, I worry, so she humors me and calls every week, just to let me know she's doing okay. But I haven't heard from her lately, and now, she's not answering her phone. When's the last time you saw her?"

McTavey frowned, searching back in his memories, as if every day was the same and he was trying to distinguish one from another. "A few nights ago. She worked closing. I haven't seen or heard from her since."

"She didn't contact you to say why?"

McTavey shook his head. "No. But I figured she'd just moved on. I knew it was only a matter of time."

"Why do you say that?"

"When she came in, looking for work, she told me it was a temporary thing. I expected her to give me some warning, though." His brows pulled together as if just realizing something might be amiss.

"Do you know where she was staying?"

"Above Torito's store over on 8th Street. The store's been closed for years, but the nephew rents out the upper floors on a month-by-month basis."

Zeke finished his beer and set the mug back on the bar along with a hefty tip, and then he thanked Mick McTavey and walked back out into the open air. The old guy hadn't been very helpful, but then Zeke hadn't really expected him to be. Robin Hood was smart. She knew leaving a minimal footprint was part of the game.

Dusk was settling in, lending a bit of color to the otherwise gray sky. No doubt the paper mill upriver had a lot to do with that. It operated twenty-four hours a day, seven days a week, spewing dirty smoke into the air and probably dumping toxic waste into the water.

Which, of course, was exactly why Robin Hood had chosen to come to Parryville.

The building where she lived was narrow, three stories, with an alley running between it and the carbon copy of it to the right. The first floor looked like it had been a mom-and-pop store once. A peek inside the grimy display windows on either side of a central door revealed empty shelves and a bare counter toward the back.

Chances were, the second and third stories had once been the living quarters for the family who ran the business. Robin Hood occupied the second floor. Indications were that the third floor was as empty as the first.

Zeke bided his time, circling around the building several times before disappearing into the lengthening shadows across the street. He noted the placement of windows, doors, the rickety-looking fire escape. It seemed ridiculous that someone who siphoned off millions would want to live in near squalor, but he supposed that was the point. If she waved cash around, someone was sure to notice. But if she lived in poverty, people would avert their eyes.

Spotting the pattern wasn't difficult, not once he knew what to look for. He believed Robin Hood was working from a list—one compiled from other lists, such as the worst places to live in terms of crime or health risks, where corporate conglomerates created the biggest threats to the environment, areas where things like poverty, crime, and corruption were the norm.

He did much the same thing himself, though with far less premeditation. Every place had its share of crime and corruption. He could find work in any tat shop, and within days, he would know who the players were and how they played the game. Only then would he decide if and when he wanted to get involved and to what extent.

Zeke moved among the shadows, through the narrow alley and into the tiny, overgrown patch that might have been called a backyard at some point.

He looked up, frowning when he spotted the open window.

He pulled his dark hoodie tighter around him and proceeded to the covered external staircase leading to the second floor. His plan: to get into Robin Hood's apartment, assess the situation, and then figure out where to go from there.

The first thing he noticed: the door wasn't sitting completely flush in the frame. That didn't mean anything in itself. A lot of these old places settled over time. But the cold tingle at the back of his neck suggested something else.

Zeke drew his weapon and moved swiftly and quietly to the second-floor landing. His chest constricted when he reached out with a gloved hand and found the door to her apartment unlocked.

He stepped into the darkness, giving his eyes a moment to adjust while wishing he still had his night vision goggles.

The hell with it, he thought and flipped on the light.

To the left, a living area. His eyes quickly took in the details of the room. Shabby furniture, no personal items, nothing blatantly amiss. He worked his way through the apartment, verifying that it was unoccupied.

Further back, a bedroom. The full-size bed was unmade, the coverings rumpled. A mug sat on the side table, half-full. He lifted it to his nose, recognizing the subtle scents of coconut and vanilla.

Minimal clothing—two pairs of jeans, half a dozen t-shirts, and practical undergarments—had been left in the drawers, clean and neatly folded.

He moved to the bathroom, where the faint aroma of something herbal and citrusy lingered. Lifting the bar of soap from the shower, he sniffed, confirming the source. On the vanity, a toothbrush sat in a cup, a tube of paste beside it, along with a contact lens case, and a woman's razor. They weren't the kind of items one would intentionally leave behind even if traveling light.

He examined the kitchen area next. Took in the small table, chipped countertops, and appliances older than he was. Opening the fridge, he saw that it was mostly empty, except for a few containers of healthy, organic stuff.

The floor beneath the open window was wet, presumably from the rain that had passed through the day before. No screen. He stuck his head out and saw the fire escape. Had she gone out that way?

He continued to look around for clues. What he *didn't* find was a laptop, phone, or tablet—things a pro hacker like Robin Hood would definitely have.

The sinking feeling in his stomach went from bad to worse, then bottomed out when he spotted the pair of black-rimmed glasses under the chair by the door.

Zeke closed his eyes and breathed deeply. Two things seemed abundantly clear. One, Robin Hood had left in a hurry, and two, she hadn't left willingly.

His gut clenched. Doing the kind of work she did, she was aware of the risks. But she was smart. This wasn't her first rodeo. She would have taken precautions.

What would I have done?

He went through the apartment a second time, this time with the mindset of a special operative. If he'd had any doubts about the woman's preparedness, they were dispelled by the smartly packed go bag secured to the underframe of her bed.

Zeke continued his search quickly and efficiently, looking in the usual hiding places—within the stuffing of seat cushions and pillows, the inside of the toilet tank, behind light and electrical fixture plates, and the hems of draperies.

He finally hit paydirt when he ran his hand over the window frame and his fingers detected an indentation. Getting down on his knees, he used his utility knife to pry at the gap between the sill frame and the wall until it popped loose, revealing an opening. Inside, he found a small square, like a flat Scrabble piece, with a QR code on it.

Zeke used his burner to scan the code. Almost immediately, an app began to download onto his phone. A *tracking* app.

Despite the gravity of the situation, his lips quirked. He liked this woman more and more.

He tucked the square into his pocket, then went back into the bedroom and grabbed her bag, slinging it over his shoulder. On the way out the door, he paused and picked up her glasses, too, leaving everything else the way he'd found it.

CHAPTER SIX

~ *Aggie* ~

THE SOUND OF MEN'S VOICES, tinged with anger and frustration, roused her. Aggie came to slowly, and with great effort, her rise to consciousness not unlike trying to swim to the surface from depths of murky, deep water.

How long had she been here? Three days? Four? Longer?

They were losing patience with her. Getting rougher. Hitting harder.

She was prone on a couch with duct tape over her mouth and zip ties around her wrists and ankles. Everything hurt. Her head pounded with a dull headache; her mouth felt as if it were stuffed with cotton. The smell of cigarettes and stale fried onions hung in the air, doing nothing to assuage her upset stomach. She forced back the nausea—the only way out was through her nose—and concentrated on gathering as much information about her situation as possible.

Aggie chanced opening her eyes to slits and

tried to focus. Without her glasses or contacts, anything more than three feet away was blurry. She was able to make out two shapes near a table and what looked like a laptop. Presumably hers.

What exactly they hoped to find, she didn't know. They didn't seem to be either particularly bright or tech-savvy.

What she did know was, there was nothing on that laptop that would interest them. She wasn't stupid enough to store anything locally, and access to the secure, private cloud server she used was only possible when certain conditions were met.

She concentrated on other things, like their voices. One sounded relatively young. The other, rougher and more commanding—and unfortunately, the one she'd tased in her apartment. The subtle melody of birdsong and the lack of traffic and people outside suggested she was no longer in the town.

"It's clean," the younger man said. "There's nothing here."

"Look again," the rougher voice commanded.

"I can, but the results aren't going to be any different. I've done a complete scan. No wire transfers, no pictures, no incriminating emails, no hidden files. Either you picked up the wrong device or you picked up the wrong girl."

The older guy grunted, then moved further into her range of vision.

"You can stop pretending now. I know you're

awake."

When she didn't respond, he grabbed her by the hair and yanked her to an upright position, which did nothing for her headache or her roiling stomach. She stared up at him with wide, scared eyes.

Cold malice rolled off him in waves. This was a man who wouldn't think twice about snapping her neck. Might even take pleasure in it.

He ripped off the duct tape, and she sucked in a mouthful of air—air tinged with men's cologne and tobacco. She squinted to bring him into better focus. He grabbed a chair and set it in front of her, then sat down on it.

"Let's try this one more time. Where are the files?"

She blinked and tried to focus past the dots swimming in her vision, responding the same way she had every other time he'd asked. "What files?"

He smiled. It was chilling. "The files that contain the information you and your boyfriend have been stupid enough to keep."

"I told you, I don't know what you're talking about. And Sam is not my boyfriend. We went out a couple of times as friends—that's all."

"That's not what he said."

She pulled her brows together in confusion and shook her head. "Then, he's lying."

He moved so fast that she couldn't have defended herself even if her wrists weren't bound. His hand shot out and hit her hard, sending her off the couch and onto the floor in a heap. She curled into a ball and tried to make herself as small as possible.

He followed that up with a swift and sudden kick to her kidney, and *holy hell*, that hurt.

Leather-gloved fingers grabbed her by the hair again and yanked her to her feet as if she weighed nothing, then he slammed her against the wall. Pain exploded at the back of her head and radiated down her spine.

He moved in close. Close enough that she could see every cruel feature. She committed them to memory. Pale, pockmarked skin. Dark, close-cropped hair and darker eyes. A wide nose that looked as if it had been broken a few times. A faint, thin scar that ran from his left ear to his jaw.

His smile grew colder. He didn't break eye contact as one large hand closed around her neck and lifted until her feet dangled several inches from the floor. Her bound hands gripped at his fingers in a desperate attempt to loosen his hold as she kicked out. She managed to land one double-footed kick before he calmly reached down, grabbed her right ankle—the same one that had been dislocated during the snatch and grab—and twisted. He punctuated that with another body slam against the wall.

Her lungs emptied in a sudden woosh, and fresh waves of pain rolled through her in both directions, from the back of her head downward and from her twisted ankle upward. The waves met in the middle in a nauseating collision.

She groaned in pain and tried to suck air back into her lungs.

His phone buzzed with an incoming text, giving her a temporary reprieve. He held her easily with one hand while he checked his phone with the other. His eyes darkened, and his scowl deepened. Then, he shoved his phone back into his pocket.

"I'll be back. You have until then to reconsider. If you refuse to tell me what I want to know, I'll start removing body parts until you do."

She believed him.

His hand tightened, causing bright lights to pop in and out of her vision. He leaned in until she could feel his breath on her face and spoke menacingly. "I'll start with your feet. Then your hands. Then your eyes."

He shoved her into the wall one more time for emphasis, then released his hold. She fell to the ground, gasping for breath.

"You," he barked, presumably to the younger guy, "keep working. If she tries anything, use the Taser. She's quite fond of it."

Her head pounded. Her cheek and jaw were numb. Her body ached all over, and her ankle was swelling around the zip tie, resulting in a loss of sensation.

Still, she'd been in worse situations.

"You should just tell him, you know," the

younger man said, his voice softer and quieter, almost soothing compared to his partner's.

Aggie squinted and made out another figure standing several feet away. He wasn't nearly as tall or as wide as the other guy. Pale. Unkempt hair but clean. Glasses. The resident geek, she presumed. He didn't have the same air of malice her abuser did, but he didn't seem particularly bothered by violence either.

"I told you, you must have me mistaken with someone else. I'm a bartender at McTavey's."

"Bartenders don't have five-thousand-dollar laptops."

"They do if they steal them from their cheating, drug-dealing ex," she said on a groan.

He snorted. "You expect me to believe that?"

"Look, I stole the thing and ran, okay? Why else would I be hiding out in a place like Parryville and working under the table for lousy tips? I don't know what's on there, only that it was important to him."

"What's your ex's name?"

"I can't tell you. He'll kill me."

"If you don't, *he'll* kill you," the guy said, inclining his head toward the door where the other guy had gone through.

Aggie thought back on the names she'd gathered over the last couple of months, searching for one that might instill fear in a lower-level grunt. "If I tell you, will you cut the ties around my ankle?

I can't feel my toes."

He looked at her feet, his brows pulling together, as if considering it, then shook his head. "I can't."

"Dude, look at me. Look at my ankle. It's not like I'm going to be running anywhere."

When he continued to shake his head, she called forth the waterworks. Aggie wasn't above shedding a few tears. She needed him within arm's reach, and time was of the essence. She had no idea when the other guy was coming back, and once he did, escaping the situation would become considerably more challenging. This might be her only chance.

"Please. Just … get me some ice or something. That's not against the rules, is it?"

This time, he nodded. He went over to an ancient-looking refrigerator and pulled two ice trays out of the freezer. He opened a few drawers, found a box of plastic zip bags, and popped the cubes into one.

Aggie did her best to look defeated or, at the very least, nonthreatening. She made a show of struggling to sit up. He helped her, his touch much less abusive than that of Harvey Wallslammer's.

"Thanks," she said softly, sniffling.

His lips thinned, but there was a flash of sympathy in his eyes.

When he turned his gaze downward to put the bag of ice on her ankle, she jackknifed forward and looped her bound wrists over his head. At the same time, she raised her knees and smashed them into his face. She tugged around his neck, keeping up enough pressure to restrict his flow of oxygen. He struggled, but she used leverage until he went slack.

When she was sure he was out, she released her grip and heaved him to the side. Then, she crawled, hungry-caterpillar style, toward the kitchen in search of a knife. She had no idea if more men were stationed outside.

One thing at a time, Aggie. Being armed and unbound was her immediate goal.

She pressed her back against the cabinets and pushed on her feet, gritting her teeth against the pain that shot up from her ankle, until she was standing, leaning heavily against the counter.

She found a steak knife and propped it vertically in a drawer, using her body weight to hold it upright and in place while she sawed away at the zip ties around her wrists.

She'd just cut through when her senses went on high alert. Someone was disabling the lock.

Aggie dropped back down to the floor, and frantically went to work on the ties around her ankles. If she could stay out of sight long enough to free her legs, she'd be in a better position to defend herself.

The door opened slowly. A figure entered, stopping just inside the room. Aggie squinted to see who it was. It was a large man, not one she recognized. His arms were outstretched, as if holding a weapon, and he began working his way across the space toward her. He was big, his movements powerful and graceful. She stayed on the floor, barely daring to breathe as she gripped the knife. It wasn't much in terms of an effective weapon, but it was all she had. Combined with the element of surprise, it would have to be enough.

The newcomer crouched down, checked out the geeky guy on the floor, then stood again, and turned in a circle.

It didn't take long for him to spot her. He moved forward, his steps quicker than they had been but still silent. "Are you all right?"

She pulled out the knife and held it to his throat. "Do I *look* all right to you?"

"I'm not here to hurt you," he said, his voice calm, as if she didn't have a blade pressing against his jugular.

"Why *are* you here?"

"To get you out, although I'm not sure you need my help," he said with the ghost of a smile. It was oddly distracting. "Are there any more besides the kid with the broken face and the two guys posted outside?"

There were two men posted outside? "One. He left, but he's coming back."

"Then, we should be gone before then. Agreed?"

Aggie didn't know who this guy was or what

he wanted, but at the moment, he was the lesser of evils and her best chance of escaping.

"Agreed."

"Then, how about we save the shave for later?"

She realized she was still holding the blade against his neck and lowered her arm.

"Here. These might come in handy." He reached into his pocket and pulled out her glasses.

She put them on and got a good look at his face. Gorgeous gray-green eyes stared back. A zing of awareness shot through her, and for just a moment, she forgot to breathe.

Not the time, Aggie. Put that adrenaline to better use.

She forced her gaze away when she felt heat rising beneath her skin and took a better look around, getting her first clear picture of where she'd spent the better part of a week. It was an old farmhouse, by the looks of it, and one that hadn't been renovated for decades, if the harvest-gold appliances were any indication.

The mysterious stranger stood and held his hand out to her. She took it, wincing when she got to her feet. Well, one foot. The other she held mostly in the air. Swollen and twisted as her ankle was, even slight pressure caused pain to shoot up her leg.

He looked down, frowning. "Can you walk?"

She gritted her jaw in determination. "I'll crawl if I have to. Just get me out of here."

He grunted skeptically but said nothing. She hobbled along behind him, pausing at the table to grab her laptop.

"Wait here," he told her. "I'm just going to make sure we don't have any new arrivals."

He disappeared, returning a minute or so later. It felt like forever.

"Sorry, but I'm going to have to override the DIY."

Before she translated his statement, he lifted her over his shoulder like she weighed nothing. She let out a gasp and grabbed at his shirt, intent on holding on and trying not to think about the steel bar of his arm pinned against the back of her thighs. He moved with swift, long strides, taking them into a copse of trees far faster than she could have gotten there herself.

He placed her into the front seat of an older-model sedan. The steering column was already apart, suggesting he'd hot-wired it once. He did so again with remarkable speed and efficiency. They turned onto a two-lane road, took the first right, then accelerated when the road straightened out.

"Get down," he commanded.

"Wh—" she started when his large hand shot out and palmed the back of her head, pulling her down until she lay prone in the front seat, her face pressed against his thigh. A very muscular thigh. She thought about biting it in principle.

"Sorry," he apologized several long moments

later when he removed his hand. "I think we just passed your friend."

Aggie twisted in the seat, wincing at the pain in her back and neck, watching as a black car drove back toward where they'd just come from.

"Who *are* you?" Aggie asked. "Who sent you? And how did you find me?"

CHAPTER SEVEN

~ Zeke ~

FAIR QUESTIONS, ALL OF THEM, asked in a steady, clear tone. She was handling the situation remarkably well for someone who'd just been abducted and roughed up.

"Name's Zeke. And I found you with this." He reached into his pocket and extracted his burner phone with the location app still running.

She looked at it, then at him, her eyes narrowing in suspicion. "How did you get this?"

"I found it in your apartment."

"*Why* were you in my apartment?"

"I was looking for you."

Her eyes widened at his easy admission. He could have lied, but he preferred to avoid that if possible. Something told him that prudent honesty would hold more weight with her than bullshit.

She opened her mouth to ask the next obvious question—*why*—but he held his hand up.

"Later, okay? Let's get somewhere safe first."

"I have questions."

"I'm sure you do, and I'll answer what I can—when we're safe. Right now, the only thing you need to know is, I'm not the enemy here."

"Why should I believe you?"

He fought the urge to smile. "You mean, besides the fact that I just rescued you from your abductors?"

Her mouth formed into an adorable moue. "Yes, besides that."

"If my actions aren't enough to convince you, I doubt my words will be."

She considered that for a moment, then exhaled. "Fair enough."

"Let me ask you this. What are your instincts telling you?"

"That, at this moment, you're the lesser of two evils."

"Works for me."

His lips began to curl, and then he glanced at her and was sobered by the blossoming purple-and-black marks around her eyes and throat. He'd seen plenty of injuries over the years, but seeing them on her delicate features affected him more than most.

"Do you have anything that requires immediate medical attention?"

"No. Just a splitting headache, a messed-up ankle, and a boatload of bruises. I got off lucky."

"Most people wouldn't call that lucky."

"Would've been a lot worse if you hadn't shown up when you did. I suppose I should thank you for that."

"No thanks necessary, but you're welcome."

She said nothing more, opting to take note of her surroundings instead. Zeke knew she was probably cataloging landmarks and paying attention to the signs along the road. He could feel her shooting side-eye glances his way occasionally, too, wondering what his deal was. If she had jumped from the frying pan into the fire.

Smart woman. But then again, he'd already known that about her. He hadn't expected her to be so ... he searched for the proper word ... magnetic. Even hurt as she was, an energy buzzed around her, filling the car's interior and ghosting over his skin. And when he'd touched her? It had been like completing a circuit, that weird energy coursing into him. It had been unexpected and ... unnerving.

He'd have to make a point not to touch her again.

They drove for a while, long enough to put a decent distance between him and the farmhouse. Thankfully, she nodded off somewhere along the way. He was surprised she'd lasted as long as she had. She was a tough little thing.

Once they neared the state line, he selected a midrange hotel among other midrange hotels, one with enough similar, common, nondescript cars in the lot that they'd blend in. He swung around to the rear of the building and backed into a parking place so the plate wouldn't be easily seen, and then he gently roused her.

She blinked at him with sleepy eyes. "Where are we?"

"A hotel. We'll be safe here for the night."

"We?"

He slipped on a team cap and a pair of glasses, then reached into the backseat, where he pulled something out of a bag. "I'm going to get us a room. Do me a favor and wait here. If you don't, it'll waste time and effort, and *that* will make me cranky."

Her lips quirked. "Well, we certainly wouldn't want that."

He got out of the car and shrugged into a lightweight zippered hoodie, one large enough to conceal the finer details of his build. He walked away, hoping she heeded his words. Surely, she had to know that if he'd planned on hurting her, he could have done so multiple times.

He procured a room easily enough. When he returned, he was disappointed to see that she wasn't in the passenger seat, where he'd left her. He'd just resigned himself to go after her when she popped up from behind the car and he realized what she'd been doing.

"The plate number won't tell you anything about me," he told her matter-of-factly.

"It'll confirm you're a car thief."

He sighed. "I prefer the term *borrowed*."

She huffed, then asked, "Did you get a room?"

"Yes."

"Good. I need ibuprofen, a hot shower, and food—in that order. Then, you can start answering those questions."

"Are you always this bossy?"

"Yes. It's one of my more endearing qualities."

He stifled a smile as he pulled the large bag out of the back and looped it over his shoulder. Her spirit and practicality were admirable.

They entered the building through a side entrance. When he saw a rather large group waiting for the elevator, he guided her into the stairwell instead. The less people they came in contact with, the better. Ignoring her feeble protest, he scooped her up and carried her to the third floor. His inner caveman wouldn't allow him to watch her hobble up two flights on a bad ankle even if he had made up his mind not to touch her again.

"White knight complex, huh?" she said, her eyes holding amusement as she looped one arm around his neck and shoulders.

"No. I'd just like to get into the room before dawn."

She huffed softly. He gritted his teeth and ignored the feel of her body pressed against his.

He'd chosen their room carefully, equidistant from the stairwell and elevator, at the back of the building with a view of the lot. Once inside, he quickly deposited her on the bed farthest from the door. He removed the large bag from his shoulder, then reached in and extracted a smaller one.

"My stuff!" she exclaimed, recognizing the go bag he'd lifted from her apartment during his search.

"I grabbed it when I went to your place. Thought it might come in handy."

Looking thrilled, she picked it up and hobbled toward the bathroom. "A pierced and tatted white knight who thinks ahead. Be still my beating heart. Sorry, I'm calling first dibs on the shower. Can you get us something to eat? Something semi-healthy if possible."

She didn't wait for him to answer before closing the door behind her. Shaking his head, he searched out local delivery options, then placed an order for something he thought she'd like. That done, he proceeded to secure the room by ensuring the windows were locked, closing the blinds, and placing weapons out of sight but within reach.

Then he called Charley. "I've got her."

"Good." Charley provided the address of a safe house several states away and told him to call again when they were twenty-four hours out.

By the time Robin Hood emerged from the bathroom in a cloud of herbal-scented steam, the food was waiting, and the door had been secured for the night. No one was getting in or out without him knowing about it.

Her eyes lit up when she saw the vegetable stir-fry he'd selected—the closest thing to healthy he'd found among nearby places that delivered. The purple-and-black shadows around her eyes and neck were deepening, but the swelling had gone down considerably, and some of the color had returned to her face. He made a mental note to pick up a pair of sunglasses if she didn't already have some.

He handed her the bag of ice he'd filled from the vending machine and the first aid kit he carried with him, then took his turn in the bathroom, secure in the knowledge that if she did try to flee, she wouldn't be able to get far.

Thankfully, it didn't appear that she had. When he emerged, she was propped up on the bed, laptop across her legs, with the television on a national news channel and a half-eaten plate beside her. She'd already wrapped her ankle, and she had it elevated, which he found slightly disappointing. He wouldn't have minded doing that for her, then shook off that unhelpful thought. Their time together would end the minute he got her to the safe house. The less reliant on him she was, the better.

Her eyes swung over to him, widening slightly as she checked out his chest and then, when he turned, the intricate tats that adorned his torso and back. That lifted his spirits somewhat.

He pulled on a T-shirt, hiding a smile at her obvious disappointment, then approached her bed and curled his fingers in a silent request to hand over her laptop. "Not smart."

She twisted, pulling the laptop out of his reach.

"It's secure."

"Yeah? Then, how did those guys find you?"

"I don't know, but I can tell you, it's not because of this." When he continued to look skeptical, she said, "That's not how *you* found me, is it?"

"Technically, it is," he countered.

She waved her hand dismissively. "Because you found the GPS locator I put on it in case it got stolen. What made you go to my apartment in the first place? You said you were looking for me. Why?"

He sat down on the other queen, the one closest to the door, and grabbed a covered plate. He took several bites, ignoring her penetrating stare. She was tough and cute, but she needed to understand that he did not answer to her and that any information he provided would be at his discretion, not her demand.

"You said you'd answer my questions when we were in a safe place," she reminded him. "This is a safe place. So, start talking."

He took his time and another few bites, then downed a bottle of water and wiped his mouth. Only once he was finished eating did he deign a response.

"I was hired to find you."

"By whom?"

"A woman named Charley."

Her face scrunched up. "I don't know any

woman named Charley."

"Well, she knows you."

"Got a last name?"

"Just Charley, and I doubt that's her real name. I've never met her. We've only spoken on the phone."

She considered this for a moment. "Her name is Charley, and you've only spoken on the phone. Your last name isn't Bosley by any chance, is it?"

He felt his lips quirk. "No. And in the interest of accuracy, *that* Charley was a man."

"We don't know that. Voices can be easily simulated," she countered with a sniff. "So, what are you, some kind of mercenary bounty hunter or something?"

"Or something."

Another scrunchy face. She didn't like that answer, but that was all she was going to get.

He crossed his arms. Her eyes flicked to his biceps, and then she blinked.

"Why did this Charley hire you to find me?"

"Your sudden and unexpected disappearance raised some red flags."

"What flags?"

He ignored her question. He couldn't think of a good way to answer it without spooking her more than she already was. "Charley feels you perform a useful service, and apparently, she'd like it to continue."

Her pretty hazel eyes narrowed suspiciously.

With the black rims framing the dark bruises, she reminded him of a little raccoon. "What useful service?"

"You tell me, *Robin Hood*."

She blinked, then shook her head. "*Aggie*. My name is Aggie."

"That's the name you've been using for the past six months, but it's not who you really are."

"Oh? And who am I?"

"You're the woman single-handedly responsible for blowing the whistle on at least two dozen scams in the past five years and siphoning millions into various charities around the country."

"What color is the sky in your world?" Her expression was incredulous, but the gleam in her eyes gave her away.

He laughed. He liked her more by the minute.

"I hate to break it to you, Zeke—if that is your real name—but I'm a bartender and not a particularly good one at that."

That might be true, but it wasn't all she was. Nor was it a denial that she was Robin Hood.

"Bartenders don't have go bags under their bed and tracking tiles concealed in windowsills, and they don't get abducted by thugs."

She raised her eyebrow and looked pointedly at him. "And yet, here we are."

"I'm not a thug," he protested. "And I didn't abduct you."

"So, you'll just let me walk out the door

anytime I want?"

"No, but I'm not going to hurt you either."

Her head tilted to the side as she regarded him. "So, let me see if I have this right. Someone I don't know noticed I wasn't around, figured me to be this mythical Robin Hood character, and hired you to find me."

"That about sums it up."

"What do you get out of it?"

"Money."

She pulled her knees up to her chest—a subconscious, protective gesture—a look of disappointment on her face, and said nothing for several long moments.

"What are you supposed to do with me now that you've found me?"

"Get you to a safe house."

"And then what?" she pressed.

He shrugged. "Then, my job is done."

"What about me?"

"That's between you and Charley."

More seconds passed by in silence before she said softly, "I think I misjudged you, Zeke."

He felt some of the weight that had settled in his chest begin to lift, and then she added, "You aren't the white knight type at all, are you? You're just a mercenary whose priority is putting a few bucks in your pocket, hired to do a job, and to hell with everything else."

Zeke kept his expression neutral despite the

direct hit. This woman knew nothing about him and had said the one thing that cut right to the heart of the matter—to the heart of *him*—because she was right. He had once been that guy. The one who obeyed orders, did what he was told, trusted his so-called superiors when they said they'd have his back.

But he wasn't that guy any longer.

He didn't tell her that he'd asked all the questions. That he hadn't taken the job because of the money. That he'd done it because of *her*. Because of something in her eyes that had latched on to him like some kind of multi-pronged, barbed hook and hadn't let go.

"What if I don't want to go with you?" she asked.

He didn't answer. He didn't have to. He saw the moment understanding dawned, dimming the light in her eyes. She was as much a prisoner now as she'd been in that farmhouse. The primary difference was, he had no intention of harming her. His job was to keep her safe.

"I see," she said after several long moments ticked by in tense, uncomfortable silence. Something wasn't adding up.

"Why did those guys take you? What *did* they want?" he asked.

"They asked me where the files were."

"What files?"

"I don't know. They seemed to think I was

working with someone."

"Working with who?"

She shook her head. "I don't know."

Zeke's instincts told him she wasn't lying, but it seemed like too much of a coincidence to believe otherwise.

"You should get some rest," he said gruffly, leaning back on the pillows. "We've got a long day ahead of us tomorrow."

"I will—soon. I just need to check a few things first."

"What things?"

She offered him a small smile that didn't reach her eyes. "What do you care? That's not your job, right?"

Her attention went back to her screen, but she'd already scored a second direct hit.

CHAPTER EIGHT

~ *Aggie* ~

ZEKE APPEARED TO BE SLEEPING, but Aggie suspected the possum routine was meant to lure her into a false sense of security. She had no doubt that if she tried to make a break for it, he'd be on her before she made it to the stairwell.

A freaking mercenary. It figured.

She was disappointed, but not surprised. Hot, gorgeous men didn't ride in on white horses to save the day, not unless they were being paid to do so.

Not that she needed saving. She'd been on her own for a long time, and she could take care of herself. Mostly. Occasionally, the universe liked to throw in a wrench or two, just to keep her on her toes.

The last few days were a perfect example. She still didn't know what her unfortunate snatch and grab had been about, but she didn't believe it'd had anything to do with her covert digital activities. As much as she didn't like admitting it, Zeke's timely arrival had made things much easier.

What happened next, that required some thought. Without knowing who or what awaited her, it was impossible to make an informed decision. However, allowing herself to be delivered to someone who hired mercenaries probably wasn't in her best interests.

As for Zeke, she was usually pretty good at reading people, but he was a challenge. Chivalrous, but mercenary. Accommodating, but not friendly. Hot AF, but not full of himself. He was clearly skilled with a definite special ops vibe pulsing just below the surface.

Maybe he worked for her brother?

She didn't know why it hadn't occurred to her before. It would explain how he'd found her. Very few organizations had the resources to track anything back to her, and her brother's was one of them.

It wasn't as if T could openly acknowledge her, no more than she could, him. Their lives—and the lives of others—depended on it. Their communications were necessarily few and far between, and when they did happen, they were only done through a private and extremely secure process.

Which meant she had to get to one of *her* safe houses because if T *wasn't* behind this, then it could be devastating for both of them.

She tapped away at the keys, verifying her digital lurkers continued to run like a finely oiled machine, and considered her options. Slipping away wasn't feasible. Her sexy mercenary was too alert, and physically, she needed another day or two to recover before she struck out on her own. For now, playing the role of the reluctant but resigned package was the way to go.

Aggie closed the lid of her laptop and yawned. She was tired and sore, but at least she was clean, well fed, and for the moment, safe. Clutching her laptop to her chest as if it were a teddy bear, she turned on her side—the one with the least amount of aches and pains—and tried to get some sleep.

She managed an hour, maybe two, before something woke her. She remained still, opening her eyes and ears and listening intently. The room was dark, but she sensed movement. She wasn't alone, and it took her a moment to remember why.

"Relax," said a deep voice from over by the window. "It's just me."

"How did you know I was awake?"

His response was a soft chuckle, one that made her shiver—and not in a bad way. She couldn't see him, but she could feel his eyes on her. Despite being under the covers, she felt exposed. And oddly aroused.

"Right," she breathed, sitting up and swinging her legs over the side of the mattress, irritated with herself.

Finding him attractive was one thing. Dreaming about him and enjoying the feel of his eyes on her were another.

So irritated was she that she forgot to factor the soreness of her twisted ankle when she put both feet on the floor and tried to take a step. She grunted and lurched forward ... right into a hard, shirtless body. Strong arms gripped hers, sending rippling tingles ghosting over her skin.

"Easy there."

"I'm fine." She pushed him away and limped to the bathroom with gritted teeth, relying on memory with her arms stretched out in front of her. She didn't bother turning on the light. She knew where everything was.

When she reemerged a short while later, the room was still mostly dark, but he'd moved the shade slightly to the side. A small amount of light filtered into the room, allowing her to make it to the bed without further incident. Once between the sheets, Aggie caught sight of his outline by the window briefly before the shade closed and the room was once again enveloped in blackness.

She listened. Heard nothing from within the room, only muted sounds from outside.

"Is Zeke your real name?"

A hesitation and then, "Yes."

"So, what are you anyway? Green Beret? SEAL? MARSOC?"

"None of those things," he said quietly.

"But you were, weren't you?"

His silence was as good as a confirmation.

"What happened?"

"Go back to sleep. We leave first thing in the morning."

If he thought his nonanswers would dissuade her from wanting to discover more, he was mistaken. She was more intrigued than ever.

"What about you?" she pressed. "Shouldn't you get some rest too? Assuming you'll be doing the driving, that is. I can sleep in the car, but you need to stay alert, especially since you're the only one who knows where we're going. It'd be a shame to go through all this just to wind up wrapped around a tree because you dozed off."

A snort.

"I promise I won't try to escape tonight," she added softly. "Get some rest, okay?"

A sigh. Then the barely imperceptible shift of air and the sound of him settling onto the other bed.

She smiled into the darkness, surprised that he'd acquiesced so easily. Maybe there was hope for him yet.

Aggie didn't think she'd be able to fall back asleep right away. Her mind was whirling with thoughts of the mysterious man she was sharing a hotel room with. *Who was he? What was his backstory? What had made him become what he was?*

And why did she feel this instant, annoying attraction to him?

Granted, he was tall, dark, and gorgeous and

had amazing eyes. He had an aura of danger surrounding him and had been chivalrous enough to carry her up two flights of stairs.

She thought of his strong arms and being held against that warm, hard chest—the one covered in beautiful, intricate tattoos—and felt something stirring within her. Had they been in a romance novel, they would have fallen into bed, crazed with lust, and spent a passion-filled night making each other see God.

Aggie shook those thoughts off when heat began pooling uncomfortably between her legs. They weren't characters in a romance novel, and the reality wasn't nearly as sexy. Yeah, he was a fuck-hot bad boy who pushed her buttons *in theory*, but the reality was, he was a glorified bounty hunter, working for God knew who.

That cooled her burgeoning desire and had the added benefit of reminding her that the only person she could trust was herself. At some point, an opportunity to part ways would arise, and when it did, she was going to take it. She needed to contact her brother and figure out what was going on.

It was a pity they couldn't partake in some hot and sweaty monkey sex along the way though.

* * *

When Aggie opened her eyes again, it was morning. The curtains were still drawn, but the sun was bright enough to backlight them and brighten the room.

She reached for her glasses and peered around. There was no sign of Zeke. His bed was made. The bathroom door was open, the small room unoccupied. It was a shame she didn't feel good enough to make a break for it just yet.

It was most likely a test. He was probably skulking outside the room, waiting to see if she'd try to run.

Sorry, Zeke. No running today.

She hobbled to the bathroom and did her business, and then she took more ibuprofen and another shower, letting the pulsating hot water temporarily ease some of her aches and pains. When she emerged a short while later, fully dressed and feeling slightly better, Zeke still hadn't returned, so she sat cross-legged on the bed and began her morning meditation.

Zeke entered just as she was finishing up her intentions for the day, which included giving herself permission to take it easy and finding out as much as she could about her escort and his mission. He didn't seem surprised to see her, which meant either he had been skulking or he trusted her. She didn't think it was the latter.

His eyes lingered on her with an unreadable expression before they moved to her already-packed bag. "Good. You're ready to go."

She unfolded herself with care. "Where were

you?"

"Getting us a new ride."

"Stealing another car?"

"*Borrowing.*"

She snorted.

"Where did you think I was?"

"I was kind of hoping you went for breakfast."

His lips quirked as he tossed her an apple and a banana. "Complimentary breakfast. We'll get something more substantial once we put a few miles behind us."

He took the bag from her hand and stuffed it into his own before slinging it over his shoulder. He reached for her next, but she stepped back. The thought of being held against that broad, hard chest was a pleasant one, but she had to keep her wits.

"I'd prefer to walk, if you don't mind."

If his expression was anything to go by, he did mind. In fact, she thought she saw a flash of disappointment there as well. But he exhaled and nodded, and those rose-colored lenses she was wearing went back to normal.

Leave those romantic notions to the romance writers, Aggie. You're just a paycheck to him, and you'd do well to remember that.

CHAPTER NINE

~ *Zeke* ~

SHE HADN'T TRIED TO GHOST, which surprised him. Then again, she wasn't really in the condition to do so. She was moving slowly and with great care.

Not that she would have gotten far even if she were at one hundred percent.

He held the door open for her, and she limped past him. Aggie immediately turned toward the stairs.

"Don't you want to take the elevator?" Zeke asked, looking pointedly down at her ankle.

"No. I try to avoid them."

"Why?" he asked before he could stop himself.

She huffed. "Does it matter?"

"It does if I need to factor that into an exit strategy."

"You don't. I can ride them. I simply prefer not to."

She hobbled a few more steps, then shot over her shoulder, "I saw a horror movie when I was a kid about a possessed elevator car, okay? I still can't get into one without thinking about it."

"Okay," he said, surprised by the fact that she'd shared that with him.

The stairwell was narrow enough that even her petite arms could reach the bars on both sides. Zeke's heart stopped several times as she gripped the handrails and swung her way downward several steps at a time, keeping the weight off her bad leg. She grinned cheekily at him when they reached the bottom.

He grunted softly in grudging appreciation, careful not to let on how impressed he was. He'd always had a thing for lithe athletic types. They were usually flexible and had incredible stamina.

He shut those thoughts down pronto. He was already walking a fine line where she was concerned. It was important to keep things professional, especially since their time together was limited. Three days to get to the safe house under optimal conditions, with minimal rest stops, good weather, no tie-ups, and changing vehicles once per day. Then, she'd be Charley's problem, and he'd have enough cash to hold him for a while, maybe even put a down payment on a tattoo shop of his own somewhere.

Sure, there was money in what he was doing, but he didn't like the way it made him feel. He especially hadn't liked the way Aggie had looked at him the night before when he told her about

Charley, as if he were the bad guy. He wasn't.

"Wait," he called out as she pushed at the exit door.

She paused and looked back at him expectantly.

He held out a pair of sunglasses. "Here."

"That bad?" she asked softly.

"Less likely to draw attention. Someone might think I'm the one who gave you those bruises and decide to play Good Samaritan."

"Yeah, that would be a shame, huh?" she said as she donned the glasses and moved into the sunlight.

He didn't know if she was kidding or not.

He led her across the parking lot to a different car, one he'd pinched earlier when she was dead to the world. He smiled, thinking of the way her tiny body had somehow taken up the entire queen-size bed. She'd kicked off all the covers and had been lying spread-eagled, her mouth hanging open, drooling onto the pillow, and snoring softly.

They got on the highway and crossed the state line. A short while later, he pulled into a fast-food place and ordered several items from the breakfast menu.

"You really know how to spoil a girl, don't you?" she said with a smirk, bypassing the breakfast sandwiches in favor of yogurt and granola.

He envisioned reaching over, pulling her to him, and kissing that sassy mouth. The image appeared so suddenly and in such vivid detail that it startled him. Instead, he focused on getting back onto the road and making short work of his bacon, egg, and cheese biscuits.

They ate and sipped coffee in relative silence, the constant hum of the tires eating up the miles beneath them. She gathered the remains and stuffed them into the takeout bag.

"How does Charley know about me?" she asked.

He wondered what had taken her so long to ask. As someone who lived in the shadows himself, it would have been the first question on his mind. Then again, the last twenty-four hours had been chaotic, and she hadn't been in the best shape.

"I get the feeling Charley knows a lot of things," he said honestly, thinking about those initial communications.

"Do you work for her often?"

"No, this is a first."

"Why?"

"I thought we covered this. She hired me to find you."

"Yes, but why did she choose *you* if she's never worked with you before?"

He'd wondered the same thing himself, especially when Charley had proven so adept at getting to him. He kept coming back to the same thing: Charley was working with someone else. Someone who trusted Charley but didn't necessarily trust everyone in her organization or want them to know about Robin Hood.

To Aggie, he said, "I'm very good at what I do."

"And finding people is what you do?"

"Among other things."

"Hmm," she hummed softly. "What else do you do besides bounty hunting?"

"What do you care?" he asked, throwing her words back at her.

She blinked, taken aback by his sharp tone. He was somewhat surprised himself.

"I don't. I'm just trying to make conversation to pass the time. Know your captor and all that."

She turned her gaze toward the window. The air in the car felt noticeably colder. He tried to put himself in her position, and the raw truth was, he didn't like the way it felt.

"Charley knew you were in Parryville," he said, breaking the silence, "as well as the fact that you went missing."

"How?" she asked, looking paler than she had just a short while earlier.

"She's quite familiar with your work. Even sent me a list of your greatest hits."

She looked skeptical, so he told her about the links Charley had sent him. Judging by the way her face paled further, he guessed she hadn't expected anyone to connect the dots and certainly not follow them back to her.

"You really don't know who she is or who she works for?"

"No, I really don't."

She went quiet again. A quick side glance showed her brows creased and her fingers flexing, as if itching to let loose on a keyboard.

He debated whether to tell her his theory, then decided she needed to know. He liked her. Liked her spunk and her style. Recognized a kindred spirit. Maybe, just maybe, the knowledge would help her evade detection in the future. Based on what he knew, the woman was as much of a nomad as he was, and that feeling of being trapped and hunted, well, he wanted her to have options.

He cleared his throat. "I don't know how you came to be on Charley's radar, but I think I know how you stayed on it."

"How?"

"You have a pattern."

"I do?" she asked, surprised.

He nodded. "Most people do. We're creatures of habit. And whether you realize it or not, you have a unique signature."

"Do tell."

She was looking at him again, her eyes burning with curiosity. He'd take that over her furrowed brow and worried expression.

"You're a skilled hacker, right? There's not a digital system you haven't been able to crack. Because of that, you have access to information and intel that no one outside of the highest levels of security should have."

She neither confirmed nor denied that, just waved her hand in a small circular motion for him to get on with it. "So? The world is full of hackers."

"True, but most of them use their skills for personal gain—to achieve wealth, power, a position of influence. You have a different angle, one most people wouldn't consider. You funnel ill-gotten gains elsewhere, presumably in amounts small enough to avoid detection, but never to yourself. Hence the code name Robin Hood."

"Is that it?"

He paused and glanced over at her. He could tell by the thoughtful, almost-pleased look on her face that he'd been dead-on, so he continued.

"No, there's more. Your targets set you even further apart from the others. You ignore some major cash cows and home in on others, particularly those whose crimes adversely affect the little guy. You go after those who are in a position too powerful to bring to justice through conventional, legal means. Then, you use your hacking skills to bring them down. You vary your targets, change your focus, but the pattern is there for anyone who looks close enough."

"And Charley did." She murmured the words.

"Someone else apparently did too."

Her eyes snapped up at him. "What do you mean?"

"Abduction? Farmhouse? Ring a bell?"

She shook her head. "No, I don't think so."

"Why not?"

"Because I don't think it was me they were after. I got the feeling I was more of a plan B."

"Who were they after then?"

She shook her head. "I don't know. I told you, they seemed to think I was working with someone else."

It wasn't a blatant lie, but it wasn't a full truth either. He could see her mind working, putting the pieces together.

"Talk to me. Maybe we can figure it out together."

Zeke clamped his lips shut. They weren't a team. The only thing they needed to do together was get to the safe house, then go their separate ways.

She snorted softly. "Something tells me I can't afford your help."

They rode in silence for hours. As far as road trips went, it wasn't unpleasant. She didn't chatter incessantly or bombard him with more questions or complain about the infrequent breaks, though he could tell by the way she shifted often that she was uncomfortable.

In fact, as the clock moved forward and they racked up the miles, it occurred to him that she was a little *too* compliant. He would have to stay on his toes.

They put two more states in the rearview mirror

before they stopped for the night. The trip was taking longer than it should have, what with him avoiding paid routes with cameras that would snap pictures of them as they passed through electronic scanners, but he didn't mind too much. The closer they came to completing their journey together, the less he was looking forward to it.

Like the first night, they found an unremarkable hotel. He got them a room on the second floor. He ordered food while she showered, and then secured the room once it was delivered.

When nearly forty-five minutes had passed and she hadn't yet emerged from the bathroom, the first niggling of unease began.

CHAPTER TEN

~ *Aggie* ~

AGGIE HEARD THE KNOCK on the bathroom door and ignored it. Ignored *him*. She stuck her head under the showerhead and let the pounding water massage her face and neck. The water pressure was so powerful; each drop felt like a tiny dose of acupressure on her aching muscles.

After fourteen hours in the car with her sexy mercenary, she was entitled to some private girl time.

She was attracted to him, and she didn't want to be, damn it.

The small confines of the car meant he was always there in her range of vision. It was impossible not to notice his biceps and forearms rippling each time he moved. Or his powerful thighs flexing as he worked the gas and brakes. His sculpted jaw and masculine lips had been right there within reach, begging to be touched and kissed.

He affected her in ways she hadn't been affected in a long time, which was both unhelpful and inconvenient, but it wasn't as if the powerful attraction was a conscious choice. She hadn't told her nipples to pebble or instructed the sensitive area between her legs to crave anything. They had done that all on their own.

It wasn't just his easiness on the eyes that appealed to her. It was the black ops vibe, that sense of danger lurking just beneath the surface. Also, the fact that he didn't make her cringe every time he opened his mouth, which—*bonus*—wasn't often. The man was less interested in idle chitchat than she was, and that was a damn fine trait for a man to have. She could think of far better uses for those firm male lips of his. Had, several times over the course of the day.

Would she act on those fantasies? Absolutely, she would. In fact, she already had—in the shower and by her own hand. *Twice*.

But with him? No, and she wasn't going to. He didn't need to know she'd been picturing him naked. Or imagining running her tongue along those intricate tattoos.

Knowledge was power, and he already had enough in his arsenal.

The knock sounded again—louder this time. And again, she ignored him.

Until the door opened.

She peeked out from behind the curtain and glared at him. His hand was inches from the fabric, outstretched, as if he was about to rip it open.

Where did he think she was going to go? It was a hotel bathroom. There were no windows. No other doors. There was an exhaust fan, which presumably led to ductwork, but that kind of thing only worked in the movies.

"What?" she demanded sharply.

He blinked and took a step back. "You've been in there a long time."

"*So?*"

"I …" He paused, as if at a loss for words.

His gaze raked over her bare shoulder and the visible part of her arm, moving to the area concealed behind the curtain. His eyes appeared to take on a glow.

Could he see anything through the material? Or was he just using his imagination, as she had been?

Her breasts tingled, and for one brief, insane moment, she considered opening the shower curtain and letting him drink his fill. It seemed only fair. She'd seen his bare chest after all, and she hadn't been able to stop thinking about it. Perhaps she should return the favor.

Also, she couldn't help but wonder what he would do if she did.

She didn't get the chance to find out. The tense moment lasted a few seconds. Then, he blinked again, cleared his throat, and averted his eyes.

"Food's here."

Irrational disappointment washed over her, but it was tinged with a hint of triumph, too, because his voice was huskier than it had been. Perhaps her cocky, disciplined bad boy wasn't quite as unaffected as he wanted her to believe.

"Great. Save some for me. And, Zeke?"

"Yeah?"

"Get out."

"Right."

She stayed in the shower for a while longer just *because*, then got out and dried off. Wrapping a towel around her head, she pulled on comfortable clothes and went into the main room. Zeke was sitting on the edge of the bed, staring at a television that wasn't on, looking as if he was deep in thought.

Is he thinking about me? The thought was immensely satisfying.

"It works better if you turn it on," she commented, moving to the table, where an array of takeout sat, waiting. The delicious aromas had her mouth watering, yet it didn't look as if he'd touched any of it. "Did you eat yet?"

He shook his head.

She grabbed some food and settled on the bed with her laptop. "Aw, you waited for me? That's sweet."

He grunted and frowned. Whatever she thought she might have seen on his face was gone, his expression back to the same closed business-as-usual look she'd become accustomed to. But she had seen a flare of interest—she was sure she had.

"So, how much longer until we get to where

we're going?"

"Two days. Maybe three, depending on what we hit."

An eternity. And an instant. Her window of opportunity was closing fast. She had to make up her mind. Did she continue to play the docile package to find out more about the mysterious Charley and what she was offering? Or did she disappear while she still had the chance?

She stretched her leg out, taking pleasure in the fact that Zeke noticed. Cool, collected mercenary he might be, but he was still a man who noticed a woman's bare leg.

"Tell me something, Zeke."

"What?"

"Do you do this often?"

"Do I do what often?" he asked warily.

"Work for people who want to find other people who don't want to be found."

"No."

"Why not?"

The right side of his mouth lifted in a half-smirk, half-smile. "Because I prefer to work for myself."

That was something she could relate to. "You don't work well with others, huh?"

If she hadn't been watching him so closely, she would have missed his barely imperceptible flinch.

"I don't like taking orders," he clarified.

The more time she spent with Zeke, the more

intrigued she became. He could say he was taking her to Charley for the money, but Aggie believed there was more to it than that. Deep down, Aggie sensed in him a kindred spirit, despite the fact that they came from different worlds and had different ways of doing things.

"So …," she asked, "given what you know about me, what makes you think *I* would?"

"She didn't say she wanted you to work for her," he countered. "She said she wanted you found because she feared you were in trouble. She was right."

That was beside the point. "Does she seem like the type of woman who does anything without an endgame?"

"Listen to what she has to say. If you don't like what you hear, walk away."

Aggie didn't think it would be that easy. From the little bit Zeke had revealed about Charley, the woman didn't seem inclined to accept a simple *thanks, but no, thanks* and let Aggie go on her merry way.

"If she's so easy to walk away from, why didn't you?"

"I did at first," he admitted quietly.

That was news. "Oh? What changed your mind?"

His face hardened again. "I told you."

"Right. The money."

He didn't respond to that, choosing instead to

stuff food into his mouth.

Aggie tried to focus on the latest data returned by her trollers while Zeke channel-surfed from one news station to another. He paused on a story about a Boston bank president whose body had recently been found. Initial reports suggested the guy had been shot execution-style.

"Turn that up, will you?" Aggie requested.

"The brutal murder was discovered earlier today," the reporter said into the camera. "One source close to the investigation, who spoke on condition of anonymity, said it is believed that the president of the bank, Colton Colman, siphoned millions of dollars from customer accounts, including that of reputed mob boss, Eamon Kelly. The district attorney confirmed that an investigation will be launched …"

Aggie felt Zeke's penetrating gaze.

"Did you have anything to do with that?"

Aggie frowned. "No."

Her fingers flew over the keyboard, her frown deepening. The mob boss wasn't one of her targets. If money was being siphoned from Kelly's accounts, it wasn't her doing.

But on the surface, it looked as if it was.

"You sure about that?" he asked softly.

A chill ran down her spine. Maybe it was a coincidence. It wasn't inconceivable that the bank president had gotten tired of handling other people's money and decided to skim some for himself. That kind of thing happened all the time.

But... what if there was more to it than that? What if someone familiar with Robin Hood's MO was sending a message?

The list of people who knew about Robin Hood was a short one. It included her brother—who would *never* betray her, the man currently sitting six feet away from her, and the person who'd hired him.

She could feel Zeke's eyes on her, watching her intently. The tingly feelings of attraction she'd felt earlier now became anxious butterflies in her stomach. Was this whole thing a ploy? A flex to convince her it was in her best interests to work for some secret organization? A veiled threat of what could happen if she didn't? And if so, was Zeke a willing participant, or was he simply a tool in the grand plan?

Aggie felt conflicted. Part of her wanted to believe Zeke was essentially a good guy. A mercenary, yes, but one with a code.

Another part—the part that had kept her alive in the shadows for the better part of a decade—knew it would be foolish to rest her safety and well-being on wishful thinking.

That stay-versus-go teeter-totter she was riding landed on the go side with a sudden, jarring thump.

The hard part was going to be pulling it off. The chances of getting out of this room without Zeke knowing were slim to none, which meant she was going to have to get creative.

She closed the lid of her laptop and slid it under her pillow. "It's been a long day. I'm going to bed."

She slipped under the covers and turned away from him. Her mind was racing, as was her heart. She set both to the task of finding a way out.

CHAPTER ELEVEN

~ Zeke ~

ZEKE LISTENED TO AGGIE'S steady, even breathing, but he didn't believe for one minute she was asleep.

That news story about the mob hit had spooked her—and understandably so. Still, it was the first time he'd seen her noticeably shaken. Even her kidnapping and beating hadn't affected her quite as deeply.

Which made *him* uncomfortable.

He slept lightly, balancing on the edge between full-on slumber and alertness. It would have to suffice. Only two more days, maybe three on the outside, before they reached the safe house. Then, he could return to his own shadows and sleep as long as he wanted.

The thought wasn't as comforting as it should have been.

The original reservations he'd had about taking the job resurfaced with a vengeance, along with some new doubts. He'd convinced himself that delivering the skilled hacker-slash-social-justice warrior to Charley was in her best interests. Now that he'd met her and spent some time with her, he wasn't so sure.

Everything about her was contradictory. Her quiet compliance and occasional sassiness. Her tiny, fairy-like form and her curvy, womanly features. Her inner toughness and simmering vulnerability. Her genius-level intellect and her casual ordinariness.

The most troubling thing was, the more he discovered, the more he wanted to know.

He could lie to himself all he wanted, but from the moment he'd looked into those haunted eyes, he'd wanted more.

That was some truly scary shit, especially since it was becoming increasingly difficult to keep his distance. It had taken a substantial amount of willpower not to rip that curtain open earlier and follow the path of those water droplets with his tongue. To run his hands over her toned flesh and lave every bruise until the only pain she felt was the sweet ache of desire.

There was no reason he couldn't, other than his own code of moral conduct—although, he'd consider suspending that if she expressed an interest. Several times, he'd felt her eyes on him when they were in the car, and when he'd stepped out of the bathroom, bare-chested, she'd seemed to like what she saw.

But she hadn't initiated anything, and those surreptitious glances, no matter how hot, were not sufficient to justify a seduction, and that was a damn shame. He suspected the two of them could have a good time together before they parted ways.

A soft sigh carried through the stillness, followed by the sound of covers being cast aside. Apparently, she was having trouble sleeping too. She got up several times throughout the night. Each time she did, he rose to a sense of heightened awareness, certain she was going to try to slip away.

She didn't. She visited the bathroom. Sat in the darkness by the window once or twice. Not once did she venture over to his side of the room or attempt to go near the door, so he remained where he was and said nothing.

Eventually, dawn began to lighten the edges around the windows. Zeke rose and moved toward the bathroom, where she had been for the last hour. He knocked slightly on the frame.

"Be out in a minute," came a weak reply.

She emerged a few minutes later, looking pale and tired.

"You okay?"

"I'm fine."

"You don't *look* fine."

"Thanks for the unsolicited assessment. Is it time to go?" she asked wearily, pushing past him.

"Not yet."

"Good." She crawled back into bed and curled

up into a ball, pulling the covers up to her face. "Wake me up when it is."

Then, she yawned and burrowed further under the covers.

Well, at least now, he knew why she'd been up and restless all night. Or what she *wanted* him to think. It could be a ruse. Feigning sickness was easy enough. Perhaps she thought to play upon his sympathies in the hopes of getting him to run out for something on her behalf and then disappearing when he did.

He grunted. *Not today, Robin Hood.*

Zeke pulled on the zippered hoodie and gathered his keys, and then he slipped quietly out the door and into the stairwell. There he waited, watching through the narrow rectangular window, expecting her to exit any moment.

Nothing happened. Fifteen minutes went by before Zeke went back into the room. She was still there, curled into a tight little ball, huddled under the covers, shaking.

He reached out and gently touched his fingers to her forehead. Her skin was hot and damp.

Well, hell.

She stirred, and he quickly removed his hand.

One eye opened and regarded him. "Time to go?" she asked sleepily.

"Not yet. Need anything? Want some breakfast?"

"God, no," she moaned.

"Okay. Go back to sleep."

"Okay." She closed her eyes and was out again almost immediately.

It appeared their time together would be extended for another day.

CHAPTER TWELVE

~ *Aggie* ~

MERCENARY OR NOT, Zeke wasn't immune to her discomfort. Aggie could use that to her advantage. In fact, she was quite skilled at faking illness. The white face powder and green concealer she carried in her small makeup bag were must-haves.

So far, her plan was working even better than expected. With the black eyes and the heavy bags from staying up all night, she looked like death warmed over. Toss in some shuffling feet, body curls, and soft moans, and she was very convincing. A hot, wet washcloth applied to the forehead at just the right moment clinched it.

Zeke was a smart guy—and a suspicious one. That was why she'd stuck around during his "test" exit. She needed more than a few minutes to make a proper escape.

He stuck around the room for a little while longer, then left again, presumably to get something to eat. She waited for several moments, then cautiously got out of bed.

She dressed quickly, then grabbed her bag, and slipped out. The timing couldn't have been better. Room service carts were visible in every corridor.

Aggie went up one flight, and then she ducked into an open supply closet and waited.

The woman who came in was surprised to see her and started chastising her in heavily broken English. Aggie assessed her. The woman was motherly-looking and middle-aged, with a religious pendant peeking out from her uniform—the kind of woman who might be sympathetic to someone in trouble. Aggie pointed at her bruises and pleaded with the woman to help her escape. It was almost too easy.

Soon after, Aggie was hunkered down under a pile of linens, being wheeled toward the service elevator. She felt a slight twinge of guilt, but really, it was Zeke who'd planted the idea in her head when he'd shoved those sunglasses at her.

When the linens lifted, Aggie was in the basement of the hotel, and her rescuer was speaking rapidly to a man. The man cast several looks Aggie's way, and then he nodded and beckoned Aggie toward a door.

"Go. He will see you safely away from here," the woman encouraged.

Aggie thanked her and followed the man. He handed her a jacket and cap, then ushered her into a service van. They drove out of the parking lot without incident.

"Thank you," Aggie said when he dropped her off at a shopping center several miles away.

She removed the jacket and cap and handed them back to him with heartfelt thanks. She wasn't sure he spoke any English, but he nodded and tried to shove some cash into her hand. She didn't accept it, but she did appreciate the effort.

Aggie took a deep breath and disappeared into the ebb and flow of the people moving to and from the shops, pulling anonymity around her like a favorite cloak.

She found an organic café with free Wi-Fi and ordered herself a hot cacao with coconut milk and some peanut butter energy bites. Then, she sat down in the corner and pulled out her laptop. Now that she was back on familiar footing, it was time to figure out her next move.

CHAPTER THIRTEEN

~ *Zeke* ~

A GROWL ROSE UP FROM DEEP within Zeke's chest as he took in the empty room. He'd underestimated her.

He'd *thought* she was truly ill.

He'd *thought* he'd be considerate and eat his breakfast in the nearby restaurant since even the mention of food had turned her pale complexion green.

He'd *thought* he'd positioned himself well enough to notice if she somehow tried to slip away.

Clearly, he'd thought wrong.

He verified that her things were gone, then gathered his own. She couldn't have gotten far. He hadn't been out of the room that long.

A knock sounded at the door, followed by a woman's voice declaring, "Housekeeping."

She opened the door, hesitating when she saw him standing there with a scowl on his face. She apologized and turned to leave, but he told her it was fine, that he was on his way out.

"Did you happen to see a woman?" he asked. He lifted his hand to his collarbone. "About yay high, brown hair, glasses?"

When she stared blankly back at him, he extracted Aggie's picture from his wallet and showed it to her.

The woman's demeanor changed in an instant. Her spine stiffened, her eyes narrowed, and her features hardened. "No see."

"It's important."

The woman started muttering in a foreign language, unaware that it was one he spoke fluently. She called him several nasty things, but they all painted the same picture—that he was a woman-beating piece of shit and should rot in hell.

He couldn't help but be mildly impressed. The sneaky little hacker had taken his words to heart. She'd played on the woman's sympathies and somehow enlisted her help to slip away, unnoticed.

Well played, Robin.

Zeke sighed and left the woman muttering obscenities behind him. Knowing exactly how Robin had gotten away wasn't important. Not when he still had the tracking app for her laptop on his phone.

He stepped into the parking lot and tossed his bag in his latest ride, and then he pulled up the app. Ten miles, north-northwest. Less than twenty minutes away, without traffic.

He put the car in gear and drove away, taking

his time. He was in no hurry. The dot hadn't moved. His lips curled when he thought about the look on her face when she saw him.

He turned into a town center, one with an eclectic mix of shops. The locator signal led him to an organic café tucked back in one of the corners. Zeke chose a parking spot farther away, one with a good view of the entrance, and considered his options.

Going inside wasn't ideal. All Robin had to do was cause a scene, and with her bruises, she'd be convincing. No, he was better off waiting where he was, then following her when she emerged. Once she was someplace less public, he could reclaim her and be on his way.

Ten minutes passed. Then thirty. Then an hour. A steady stream of people came and went, but there was no sign of Robin. Eventually, a niggling doubt began to make itself known.

Ensuring his cap and shades were in place, Zeke grabbed his phone and went into the café. It wasn't a big place. Besides the counter, there were no more than half a dozen two-person tables lining the right wall.

And she wasn't at any of them.

He held up the phone and moved with purpose, checking each one of the tables, ignoring the irritated reactions of those sitting there. At a table in the back, he found what he was looking for. A slim tile the size of a mini SD card, stuck to the underside of the table with … he sniffed his hand. *Peanut butter?*

"Fuck," he grumbled.

"The woman who was sitting here," he said, raising his voice to be heard among the patrons watching him with curious, wary eyes, "when did she leave?"

No one responded. If they'd caught sight of Robin's bruises, chances were, no one *was* going to respond.

Zeke cursed again, and then he moved swiftly to the exit at the rear of the store and scanned the parking lot.

CHAPTER FOURTEEN

~ *Aggie* ~

AGGIE WAS USED TO being invisible. She moved through the parking lot without drawing attention to herself, just like any other woman who didn't remember exactly where she'd parked. If that path tended to place her behind large vehicles that obscured her from anyone who might be outside the café, well, all the better.

She slipped into the shadows of one of the many brick buildings and paused to look back. Her heart was beating wildly. How could she have forgotten he had the locator app on his phone or that it was how he'd found her in the first place?

Lapses like that could get her killed … or worse. She shivered, thinking of that farmhouse goon's threat to start removing body parts as a method of persuasion. It was a completely different scenario, she knew, but this was the second time in a week she'd been caught unaware. She couldn't chance a third.

She saw Zeke step out of the café and scan the lot. She hated the way the sight of him lit her up on the inside. Hated the way part of her wanted to return to him and make the most of their final time together.

A day or two of pleasure wasn't worth the risk, no matter how sexy he was.

Besides, chances were, he wasn't too keen on her at that moment. What had he told her? That having to chase her down would make him cranky.

She smiled at that. Had the inappropriate thought of how she could get him to channel that irritation into something more pleasurable for both of them. Then, she shut those thoughts down and concentrated on what she was going to do next.

It was a shame she wasn't as adept at stealing cars as Zeke was. There were quite a few of them to choose from.

Her eyes landed on a small covered frame, partially enclosed with Plexiglas and several people waiting. A bus stop. If she could make it there, she could hop on and put some distance between her and her pursuer. She started moving again, angling herself toward the stop. Fate must have been on her side because a bus was approaching at that very moment.

She paused, watching as people got off and more got on. She blended into the waiting crowd, using a tall man as a shield.

Aggie settled in on the side farthest away from

where Zeke was. Panic tried to take hold when she realized Zeke had seen the bus, too, and was jogging toward it at a speed far too fast for her liking. The tension increased when an elderly woman getting on held things up, searching in her suitcase-sized purse for her senior citizen's ride card so she wouldn't have to pay full price.

Aggie reached into her bag and extracted enough for another fare, then moved forward and dropped exact change into the box for the woman. "I've got a job interview, and I don't want to be late," Aggie explained.

Instead of showing appreciation, the older woman sniffed and said, "Well then, I suppose you should have left earlier."

The bus driver gave Aggie a sympathetic look and closed the doors. Aggie retook her seat and searched out the window but didn't see Zeke. A bad feeling skittered down her spine and set up shop at the base and didn't relent, even as the bus began to pull away.

One step at a time, Aggie.

Zeke wasn't on the bus. That was the important thing.

Aggie exhaled, sat back in her seat, and took several discrete, deep breaths in an attempt to calm down.

Her heart raced at each of the next three stops, half-expecting to see Zeke boarding at each one. She'd already moved seats to one in the back with an emergency exit window and committed the opening instructions to memory. If necessary, she could be out within seconds.

But Zeke didn't make it onto the bus. Nor did she see him skulking around.

Yet she couldn't relax. Zeke wasn't the type to give up so easily. In fact, she realized with self-annoyance, she'd be rather disappointed if he did.

Eventually, Aggie got off the bus at a regional rail station. She lurked around for a while but didn't see any indication that she was being followed. Got something to eat. Played on her phone in the shadow of a large Ficus with an excellent view of the main entrance. Bided her time until rush hour, then blended into the wave moving toward the cars.

She boarded a train heading west and began to breathe easier when she saw the familiar landscape taking shape in the distance. The best place to hide was the place no one would ever look for her.

Home.

CHAPTER FIFTEEN

~ *Zeke* ~

SHE WAS GOOD—HE'D GIVE HER THAT. She knew how to blend in. How to be invisible.

Unfortunately for her, so did he. Plus, he had the added advantage of years of special forces experience. He could find and track anyone, anywhere.

The question he kept asking himself was, *Is it worth it?*

Several times throughout his pursuit, he thought about walking away—as much for her benefit as his. He understood her reticence about meeting with Charley. He certainly understood her distrust, though he didn't know why she felt that way. Perhaps it had something to do with why she felt compelled to do what she did—namely, a general lack of faith in a broken system.

He knew what had planted the seed of distrust for *him*—the clusterfuck that had gotten him dishonorably discharged. The same one that might have gotten him executed for treason had he not accepted their offer—claim responsibility and they'd let him walk away quietly.

His gut knotted, just as it did every time he thought about the papers he'd signed. He wasn't a traitor, not to his country, not to his team, not to anyone. And yet, he'd signed a confession that said he was.

The worst part was the look in his teammates' eyes. The disappointment. The betrayal. He'd hoped they'd see the accusations for the shams they were. That they'd recognize the whole shitshow was another government fuckup. Another cover-up. God knew, they'd been on enough ops, burying shit together. They should have known better. Goddamn it, they should have known *him* better.

Zeke exhaled and shoved the pain back, stuffing it into the box he kept locked in the back of his mind. That part of his life was over. What was done was done. Harping on it wouldn't change anything. He wasn't a SEAL anymore. He was a tattooist who moonlighted as a mercenary, and at the moment, he was getting paid to find and deliver one clever, tiny female. A female who was growing more intriguing by the hour.

He returned his attention to the task at hand, looking up at the multimillion-dollar chalet and sighed, glad that she seemed to have decided to stay put for the time being. She'd really put him through his paces with the busses and the train and finally, the Uber that had brought her here.

Soft golden light flowed from walls made of glass, spilled over cantilevered decks, and disappeared into the dense forest.

It was a far cry from the hovel where she'd been living in Parryville, which he supposed was the point. Staying unpredictable was the most effective way to remain undetected and mobile. Perhaps she'd taken his words about patterns and habits to heart.

He made his rounds around the perimeter. The chalet was remote; there wasn't another place for miles. One primary road in with two semi-concealed alternate routes along the back and sides. Strategically positioned as it was on the forested slope, it blended into the landscape and had a fantastic view of the surrounding area. The garage beneath the house held several cars, including a Range Rover and a Maybach.

A slight and unexpected pang of envy zipped through him. The isolated chalet was either the result of a wealthy recluse's paranoia or a master strategist's wet dream.

After watching and circling several times, Zeke was convinced she was the only person there. He made his way into the house on silent feet. He found her on a couch in a sunken living room, bare feet propped up on a glass coffee table. She was wearing a plush white robe, her hair wrapped up, turban-style, the ever-present laptop atop her thighs. She looked as if she'd just stepped out of a spa.

Given the size and amenities of the place, she just might have.

He stayed in the shadows, studying her reflection in the expanse of glass looking out over the mountainside. It took a full minute, maybe two, before her back stiffened and her eyes lifted, searching the glass.

Her body relaxed when she spotted his reflection, and then she exhaled heavily. Without turning around, she said, "I figured I had at least one night. You're even better than I gave you credit for, and that's saying something. Not many people exceed my expectations."

Zeke stepped farther into the room, irrationally pleased by her praise. "If it helps, you made me work for it."

"Well, I guess that's something."

She closed her laptop and shifted in her seat to face him. She looked weary. He was pretty wiped himself after chasing her all day and half the night. Tired and annoyed and oddly ... relieved to have caught up with her. She'd been a half-step ahead of him all day.

"I hope you know it's not personal, Zeke."

He nodded. His mind knew that, but based on the way his chest had loosened with her words, other parts of him didn't.

Unnerved by the softness of her gaze, he glanced around. Took in the stone hearth, exposed beams, recessed lighting. "Nice place."

"It is, isn't it? Private too."

"One of your targets' assets?"

"You could say that," she agreed, eyeing him critically. "Are you still determined to take me to Charley?"

He nodded. He didn't feel good about it, but he'd committed himself to the task.

No one said he had to drop her off and leave, however. Perhaps he'd stick around long enough to ensure that Aggie could walk away and disappear again if she didn't like whatever Charley had to say. Hell, maybe he'd go with her.

"It's been a long day for both of us, and I'm beat," she said, rolling her shoulders up and back in a graceful motion. "What do you say we take the night off and enjoy it? Indulge in a hot bath, quality liquor, and a bed that hasn't had hundreds of bodies lying on it?"

That did sound good. *Too* good.

"Why? So you can take off again?"

"I promise, no more running tonight."

"Seems I've heard that before."

"I've never lied to you, Zeke," she said softly. "And I kept my word that night, didn't I? I didn't make any such promise *last* night."

He grunted, which made her smile for some reason.

She made an X over her chest. "Cross my heart. I'm not going anywhere for at least twelve hours, maybe more. Honestly, I couldn't even if I wanted to, which, for the record, I don't."

She rose from the couch and yawned. "Whatever. I'm going to bed. You do you. Both the bar and the pantry are well stocked, so help yourself."

"How very generous of our absent hosts," he said dryly.

"That's the spirit."

She disappeared down the corridor, leaving him watching the sway of those curvy, petite hips. Hips that tugged at him like an invisible string.

Appearances were deceiving. She looked so delicate, but she was anything but. She was smart and quick and had the same fierce need to fight for the underdog as he did.

He followed the call of that sway, envisioning removing that towel and robe and climbing into bed with her while rationalizing that he was only doing his job.

He entered a spacious bedroom suite. Like the living area, it boasted an entire wall of windows with a spectacular view. A large flat screen was mounted above a stone hearth. A partially open door at the other end of the room hinted at a bathroom three times the size of the last hotel room they'd stayed in.

The massive bed on a raised dais was what drew his immediate attention, however. Draped in fluffy white bedding, it looked incredibly inviting. After several nights of only light sleep and long days of driving, he was nearing his limit.

She went over to the hearth and pressed a button, and flames sprang up. Then, she turned and arched a brow at him. "You don't trust me?"

"Forgive me if I'm skeptical."

"I guess I deserve that," she said on a sigh. "I wasn't nearly as ill as I made it seem. But if it makes you feel any better, I really did have a rough night. That dinner didn't agree with me."

"So, you lied and convinced a chambermaid I was an abusive asshole, so she'd help you escape."

She shrugged, an elegant lift of those feminine shoulders. "It worked, didn't it?"

"How'd she get you out? Linen service? Delivery van?"

Her lips quirked upward. "I'm impressed. The linen service cart took me to the laundry facility. From there, an HVAC service van took me off the premises. The HVAC guy just happened to be the maid's boyfriend. What gave me away?"

He thought about telling her he was just that good, but since she was being forthright, he could be too. "She came to do the room, and when I showed her your picture, she looked at me like I was Satan incarnate. In fact, she actually called me that in her native language."

Her tired eyes twinkled with amusement. "Educated guess, or you can actually speak Cebuano?"

He said nothing. Officially, the time he'd spent

in the Philippines had never happened.

Understanding softened her features, and she didn't pursue it. "And then you used the locator to track me to the café. Pretty sloppy on my part, huh? I don't usually make mistakes like that. Well, live and learn."

It *was* sloppy and very out of character for her. Additionally, she didn't seem particularly upset that he'd caught up to her. A niggling unease skittered down his spine. Maybe she had deliberately led him out here. Then, he gave himself an inner shake. He was overtired and overanalyzing.

"That's all you're going to say?"

"What else is there to say? I told you, I'm tired. I've been through a lot in the last week. I'm going to bed. Fair warning: if you try to drag me out of here before noon, I *will* hurt you."

With that, she stepped up to the raised bed, shimmied out of her robe to reveal a silky sheath that left nothing to the imagination, and slipped between the covers.

CHAPTER SIXTEEN

~ *Aggie* ~

AGGIE WAS AWARE OF ZEKE'S PACING well into the night, though he had to be as exhausted as she was. It went on for a while before she heard him go into the bathroom. The quick shower he took was a testament to his self-discipline. She'd lingered for much longer. Once she'd gotten under the therapeutic massage showerheads, she hadn't wanted to leave.

Of course, she knew why he'd made it such a quickie. He was afraid she was going to ditch him again. Her theory was confirmed when the first thing he did after emerging was make his way over to the bed and confirm she was still present and accounted for.

She smiled into her pillow when he grunted softly. He did that a lot. He was somehow able to manipulate the muscles in and around his throat to produce this soft, subtle, and wholly masculine sound that, in one short burst, spoke entire sentences. She interpreted this last one to convey something like, *Well, damn, she really is still here.*

Regardless, he needn't have worried. She hadn't been kidding about not going anywhere for a while. The trick was going to be getting him to stick around long enough for her to get the information she'd come for.

She heard him moving around the kitchen and breathed easier. She was glad he'd decided to unclench a little and get himself something to eat. The cupboards were well stocked with nonperishables, and the Sub-Zero had enough protein to last several months at least. The poor guy had to be hungry. Maintaining a physique that lean and muscular probably required ten thousand calories a day.

As tired as she was, sleep remained elusive. She audibly tracked his movements through the chalet. Knew that after he satisfied his immediate need for food, he would scope out all the possible entry and exit points. He might even fashion warning devices in case she tried to sneak out in the middle of the night.

Eventually, he returned to the room. He did so silently, but she didn't need sound to know he was there. She felt his presence in her very core, like a heavy static charge that hung in the air right before a powerful thunderstorm. Building. Imminent.

She could feel his intense stare, too, as he stood there in silence beside the bed, the soft pop and hiss of the gas fireplace creating soothing background noise. He was probably carefully weighing his options, deciding what to do next. There was only one bed in the suite, and she was in it. He needed rest, but he wanted to stay close, so crashing in one of the other bedrooms was a no-go.

Would he lay himself out on the floor at the foot of the bed or in front of the door? Or would the allure of a mattress and a down comforter prove too tempting to resist?

Then, she heard him grunt softly—she was really becoming absurdly fond of the sound—and felt the bed shift under his weight.

Her smile widened. The bed was big enough to hold them both comfortably. They could both lie there all night and never touch, which was no doubt what he had in mind. But the opportunity was simply too good to pass up. The hotel rooms they'd stayed in had two queens, but here, there was only one California king.

After several minutes passed, she rolled over in her feigned sleep, closer to him. Close enough to feel his body heat and fill her lungs with the scented soap from his recent shower.

She pressed against him lightly and sighed. His body stiffened, then eventually relaxed. Then, and only then, did she give in to the heavy pull of slumber.

* * *

He snored. As his heavy, powerful arm held her tightly against him, the low rumbles vibrated through her entire body. It wasn't unpleasant.

She took a few minutes to appreciate the sensation. Relished the feel of smooth skin and coarse hair beneath her cheek and thigh. The steady, strong beat of his heart and the rhythmic rise and fall of a sculpted chest.

And why shouldn't she? It had been a long time since she'd allowed herself to get close to anyone, and it probably would be an even longer period before she allowed it to happen again. She might as well enjoy it while she could.

Eventually, the call of nature grew too strong to resist, and she had no choice but to relinquish her living body pillow and heed the call. She managed to extricate herself without waking him. After taking care of personal business, she donned her robe and padded out to the kitchen in search of the two-thousand-dollar coffee machine there.

Worth every penny, she thought a short while later, sipping her first cup at the highly polished granite breakfast bar.

She fired up her laptop, unsurprised to see an urgent message from her brother.

She tapped the icon and took another heavenly sip while the secure signal ricocheted and bounced among a network of private towers and satellites across the globe, making it impossible to trace.

She hadn't yet lowered her cup when his

concerned face appeared on the screen.

"What's wrong?" he asked by way of greeting.

Her chest loosened at the sight of him, even as intense amber eyes lasered into her. Everything would be all right because her brother would make sure of it. They'd been looking out for each other for as long as she could remember. He was as protective of her as she was of him, though neither of them ever admitted it.

"What makes you think anything's wrong?" she asked easily.

"Besides the fact that you look like you went ten rounds with a UFC fighter?"

"It's not that bad. You should see the other guy."

"Seriously, are you okay?"

"I'm fine. It looks worse than it is."

He snorted.

"I'm *fine*. Listen, T, I need a favor."

"Anything."

"I need you to find out what you can about a woman who goes by the code name Charley."

He raised a perfect eyebrow, but otherwise, he didn't seem surprised by the request. "Isn't cyberstalking *your* thing?"

She shook her head. "Under normal circumstances, yes, but this is different. I'm pretty sure she's associated with a secret society. Way, way off the books. That's more your area of expertise than mine."

His eyes practically glowed. "Why are you asking about an operative?"

"She sent a mercenary to find me and bring me in for a chat."

His lips quirked. "No one finds you unless you allow it."

"Usually, that's true, but not in this case."

"Do you know why she wants you?"

"Probably for my mad skills," Aggie replied without a trace of arrogance. Her brother knew exactly how good she was. "Want to hear the weirdest thing?"

"Hit me."

"She knew where I was, and she somehow connected enough dots to associate me with prior, seemingly unrelated, socially-fortuitous events."

"That *is* weird."

Seconds ticked by in silence.

"Is Charley one of yours, T?"

"No."

"Is she a friend of yours?"

"You know I don't have any friends."

His eyes held amusement, and that was when she knew. Her brother *had* been keeping tabs on her.

"Why?" she asked. "Not that I'm not appreciative, but I thought we had an agreement not to stick our noses in each other's business unless warranted."

"We do, but this *was* warranted. You

inadvertently stumbled into a work in progress and ended up on the radar."

"How so?"

"The mill's union leaders recently appeared on the FBI's organized crime watch list. A task force was working with a source on the inside."

"What does that have to do with me?"

"Apparently, the source was a friend of yours. They were watching you and everyone else he associated with. Mostly you, because *Aggie Mays* was the wildcard they couldn't quite explain."

No wonder Sam had seemed nervous. Being a narc for the FBI was enough to make anyone tense. "Is Sam okay?"

"He went missing around the same time you did," T said. "No one's seen hide nor hair of him since. Either the FBI has him in protective custody or …" He let the sentence hang. "Are you sure you're okay?"

She nodded.

"What about the guy they sent to get you? Is he behaving himself or do I need to send a cleanup crew?"

Aggie smiled at that. "No, I can handle him. He's an honorable merc."

Her brother snorted. "He's there with you now?"

"He's very easy on the eyes."

"Seriously?"

"I know, I know," she sighed. "But he's one of

the good guys, I can tell."

Her brother's eyes went from concerned to interested, just as she'd known they would. She'd inherited the same sixth sense about people as he had. He'd no sooner disparage her instincts than he would his own.

"How good?"

"Good enough to warrant further study. He fits the profile. Thirty-something. Loner, chip on his shoulder, highly skilled. Prefers working from the shadows but definite white knight tendencies."

T hummed in interest. "Got a name?"

"Zeke, no last name given. My guess is, he's ex–special forces. SEALs, maybe Delta. I'm sending you an image now."

She tapped a few buttons and sent the picture of Zeke she'd surreptitiously captured into the ether. A soft ding sounded on her brother's end a few seconds later. He looked at it and frowned.

"Do you know him?" she asked.

"Maybe," he said noncommittally. "Let me see what I can find out and I'll get back to you. Until then, be careful."

"I will. Love you, T."

"Love you too."

* * *

Aggie didn't need to look up from her laptop to know that Zeke was staring at her from the archway. His eyes zeroed in on her like lasers, as tangible as a physical touch.

"Good morning," she said cheerfully.

"Morning," he answered roughly.

Her eyes flicked up briefly. He wore leg-hugging blue jeans and a button-down shirt that hung open, exposing ink on a lovely canvas of tight abs and tawny skin. His long hair hung loose, kissing his broad shoulders. He looked at once fierce and beautiful, rugged and comfortable in his own skin.

"The coffee's hot and strong, but if you want something other than fruit and granola for breakfast, you're going to have to make it yourself. I don't cook."

He didn't seem at all bothered by that, which was a pleasant surprise. Alpha types like him tended to have antiquated ideas of what a woman should and shouldn't do, and given the chivalry he'd exhibited thus far, she'd have put him firmly in the *women can and should know how to cook* category.

He wasted no time stalking across the space, owning it like a big, predatory cat, and then he stopped and stared at the plate of fresh fruit she'd been snacking on.

"Where did that come from?"

"Special delivery."

"How?"

"Internet. It's the latest rage. Maybe you've heard of it?"

He snorted. "Do you think that's smart? Letting people know you're squatting?"

"Who says I'm squatting? Maybe this is my place."

"Is it?"

She smiled at him benignly and blinked her eyes rapidly.

He grunted, just as she'd hoped he would. Then, he went to the fridge and foraged, pulling out a carton of fresh eggs, a sweet onion, a bell pepper, and a plate of sliced, baked ham—all recent purchases by a service paid extremely well to provide upon request.

Soon, the air filled with the delicious scents of a hearty omelet and toasted bread as he prepared his own breakfast. There was something incredibly sexy about a man who knew how to cook.

He sat down at the counter next to her. The massive omelet hung over both sides of the plate and smelled fantastic.

She clicked out of the report she'd been looking at and gave him her full attention. It could take hours for T to respond, and curiosity was eroding her patience

"That's your secret, isn't it? You're a world-renowned chef by day and get your thrills by playing badass mercenary on the side."

He scowled at her. "Playing mercenary?"

"I know it's not your day job."

"How do you know that?"

"I just do. So, are you going to tell me? Or shall I keep guessing?"

He chewed thoughtfully, as if considering whether or not to answer. Then he swallowed, drank half the coffee in one go, and said, "I'm a tattoo artist."

Her eyes roamed over the bits of ink visible on his forearms and chest, filling in the rest from the brief glimpses she'd had when he was shirtless. The pieces were breathtaking, fitted perfectly to the shape of his body. She wondered if he'd designed the tattoos himself.

"Are you any good?"

"Depends on who you ask," he said with the ghost of a smile.

"I've always wanted to get a tattoo."

"Yeah? Why haven't you?"

"Too permanent. Too recognizable," she said, waving a hand dismissively. "Especially on a woman. It's different for guys like you."

He raised an eyebrow. "Guys like me?"

She nodded. "You'd stand out more if you *didn't* have tats. You have that whole bad-boy vibe going on, which works for what you do. Hiding in plain sight, if you will. But me? I need to blend in. Working in the bar, yeah, I could get away with a few. But as a library story-time reader, not so much."

His lips quirked. "Library story-time reader?"

"You'd be surprised by the things I've done to

stay under the radar," she said.

He polished off his omelet, then pushed the plate to the side. "Not all tattoos are readily visible," he said, his eyes dipping suggestively to the parts of her currently covered.

"I suppose not," she agreed.

"If you did get one, what would you get?"

"I have no idea."

He laughed softly and called her out. "Everyone who is serious about getting ink has something in mind. Something they want."

He wasn't wrong. She *had* given it a lot of thought. She wanted something feminine. Something delicate yet strong that flowed with the natural curves of her body. Something that was unique and meaningful to her. But a specific image had remained elusive. Her creativity didn't extend to artistic things, only mathematical things, like patterns and alternate pathways.

"What would you suggest?"

He sat back and eyed her critically, like an artist eyeing a blank canvas.

"With your size and coloring, I'd go with fine line black and gray," he said finally.

"Subject matter?"

"That depends on what's important to you. It should mean something. Express who you are."

Her eyes dipped to the intricate design on his chest. Celtic and Nordic symbols, woven seamlessly into battle scenes. Bold strokes, expert shading, powerful imagery. It fit him perfectly.

"Did you design yours?" she asked, her finger reaching out to touch.

"Yes." He caught her hand, stopping her before she made contact. A jolt of energy raced up her arm and she snatched it back.

"Would you design one for me?"

"No." The answer was immediate.

"Why not?"

He didn't answer. His eyes flashed with heat before they shuttered. Then, he rose from the counter abruptly and took his dishes to the sink.

"Your little disappearing act has put us behind schedule," he said, keeping his back to her. "We should go. The sooner, the better."

"Still on about that, are you?"

"I was hired to do a job."

Aggie ignored the pang of disappointment that speared through her at the reminder. "What's wrong with sticking around for another day or two?"

He shook his head. "Not a good idea."

"Why not? We're safe here. We've got plenty of food and amenities. The view is spectacular. What's the hurry? Are you that anxious to be rid of me, Zeke?"

CHAPTER SEVENTEEN

~ Zeke ~

*J*UST THE OPPOSITE, HE THOUGHT.

The more time he spent with her, the more time he wanted to spend with her. And imagining her body splayed out before him, a perfect blank canvas upon which to permanently engrave his mark? It was pushing him to the limits of his self-discipline.

He knew he should grab her and go. But what he wanted to do and what he should do were completely at odds with one another. She was a job. A package. Nothing more.

Except she was.

So caught up was he in his mental battle that he neglected to realize she'd come up behind him. The touch of her delicate hand on his forearm was like a brand, shooting through him with a white-hot fire.

He tensed and held himself in check. *Discipline.*

"Would it be so bad, spending another day here with me?" she asked softly.

He said nothing. He was a man on the edge. He clenched his jaw and stared straight ahead and thought about the engine specs of the Harley he wanted to get someday.

"I see," she whispered, disappointment heavy in those two simple words. "I just thought …"

Whatever she thought, she didn't share it with him. She sighed and removed her hand, and then began to walk away.

Something snapped. *You can't* suddenly became *why not,* and in that moment, he needed her to finish that sentence.

She was about to take her second step when he whirled around, put both hands around her waist, and lifted her onto the counter.

Her pretty eyes widened, and she inhaled, her delicate hands clutching at the edges of his shirt, her slim, toned thighs pressing against his hips.

"What did you think, Robin Hood?" he growled.

She looked into his eyes, then tugged at his shirt, demanding he lower his torso closer to hers. But he was much bigger and stronger, and he held himself firm. If he went down that rabbit hole, he wouldn't be coming out anytime soon. Yet he couldn't move away. He was enjoying the feel of her legs around him, the scent of soft, warm woman drifting up and intoxicating him. Those big, clear eyes gazed at him with a combination of heat and desire that laid waste to his honorable intentions.

Rather than be discouraged, she ramped up her efforts. She shifted her legs upward, wrapped them around his waist, and squeezed, and she used the grip she had on his shirt to lift her butt off the counter and press her lips to his.

His hands instinctively went to support her. The moment his palms filled with the weight of her ass, his tethers snapped. He pulled her closer, taking control of the kiss.

She tasted sweet and tropical, like pineapple and coconut. Smelled like heaven. And she kissed him back as if her life depended on it.

"I've been wanting to do that for a while," she confessed breathlessly, pulling away just enough to speak the words.

"Yeah?" he replied, his voice thick and husky. "What else have you been wanting to do?"

Her grin was positively wicked as her nails scraped down his chest and over his abs, pausing meaningfully at the clasp of his jeans.

"Do you really want to know?"

Fuck yes, he wanted to know, but he couldn't say the words. He grunted instead.

For some reason, that seemed to delight her. Her lips were on his again. One hand slipped around his neck; the other slid down between them and into his jeans. She exhaled with the sexiest purr he'd ever heard when she cupped him and traced his length.

"Robin …" he hissed. Her touch was magic,

sending shock waves of desire flooding through him.

"Aggie," she whispered. "My name is Aggie. Say it."

"Aggie," he complied, internalizing the significance to unpack later. Much later.

Her hand was small but strong, and the pressure she exerted was exquisite. In a matter of moments, her shirt was off, and she was arching backward, pulling his hair as he feasted on her surprisingly lush breasts.

The desire to be inside her raged inside him, almost frightening in its intensity. Now that he released the reins, want and need collided in a massive surge. Images flooded his mind, filling it with all the things he hadn't allowed himself to think about the last few days, things that had nevertheless plagued his subconscious every time he let his guard down.

Her breasts weren't the only things he tasted. By the time she'd cried out his name twice, he was ready to explode.

Thank God he'd spotted the box of condoms in the bathroom.

He carried her there next, his only thought to experience her next orgasm while deep inside her. The moment he wrapped his package, he took her right there on the vanity.

He had known it would be good. He hadn't realized *how* good. She fit around him as if she'd been made specifically for him. Hot and wet and tight, she was the very definition of heaven. She raked her nails across his back, squeezing, beckoning, demanding more.

He gave her everything.

Because after today, he'd never have another chance.

* * *

Zeke traced the pad of his finger down the curve of her spine, then flattened his hand against her warm skin to fully experience the sensation of her delightfully lush hips. He wondered if they would show signs of how tightly he had gripped them when she had ridden them both into ecstasy.

Closing his eyes, he created an intricate, fine-lined design in his mind that would fit her curves perfectly. He fantasized about running the needle over her pristine skin and then covering her body with his, branding her inside as thoroughly as he had outside.

The fantasy would have to remain just that—a fantasy. He'd already crossed a line by sleeping with her. But he could walk away from that, difficult though that would be. If she wore his art, that would be a permanent connection between them, and that, he couldn't allow.

They'd spent most of the day naked and finding new ways to pleasure each other. They'd started in the kitchen and worked their way around the luxurious chalet, taking a detour to fuck on the open-air balcony before eventually winding up in the master bedroom.

She was exquisite and desperate, as eager to give as to receive. He guessed it had been a long time for her too. Living the kind of lives they did, finding someone to share intimate moments with was a challenge.

Correction: finding someone *worthy* to share intimate moments with was a challenge.

"Are you hungry?" he asked lazily.

She hummed and peered up at him with contented eyes. "I'm guessing you are, or you wouldn't have brought it up."

He was. Famished in fact. A man couldn't exert that much energy and not be.

She laughed, stretched up his body, and planted a kiss on his lips. "Go on then. I'm going to get a shower."

The thought of her naked and soapy and wet was enough to make him reconsider his immediate plans. Then, his stomach growled loudly, overriding his semi. He liked to think he was a virile man, but she'd pushed him to his limits, and he needed sustenance.

"Go," she urged.

She pushed off the bed and padded into the en suite. He watched, appreciating the view, then sighed and went into the kitchen.

He raided the fridge, pleased to find some prime steaks among the items she'd had delivered. He selected two, then turned the flame on the built-in grill to preheat it. He wasn't a material guy by nature, but if he ever had a place of his own someday, he would definitely have one of those.

Zeke found some potatoes and cut them into thick slices as well, and then he dumped them into a cast iron pan with more of the onion and pepper stash he'd raided that morning. As the vegetables sizzled, he cracked open a beer and took a moment to appreciate the situation.

He was warm and clean and not in immediate danger, about to fill his belly after indulging in a marathon of great sex. Days like this didn't come along often. It was important to appreciate them when they did.

A soft ding sounded from nearby. Her laptop was still on the coffee table, where she'd left it earlier. Curious, he opened the lid, surprised when the screen lit up without requiring a password.

He clicked around, feeling a sense of panic when the screen went black and a skull and crossbones appeared with the message, *Self-destruct sequence initiated.*

"Fuck, fuck, fuck," he murmured, slamming the lid closed.

He heard her soft laughter and found her grinning at him from the archway. Her hair was wet. Her skin was dewy. Her eyes glittered with mischief and amusement. She was, in that moment, the most beautiful woman he'd ever seen.

And she didn't seem concerned in the least.

"It's not going to self-destruct, is it?" he asked.

"No. There's no reason for it to. It's a conduit, nothing more."

"A conduit to what?"

"Information. You don't actually think I'm stupid enough to keep anything on my laptop, do you? That smells fabulous. Did you make enough for me?"

The abrupt change in topic wasn't lost on him, but he was in too good of a mood to spoil it.

"Maybe. You do eat meat, right?"

She smirked. "After today, how can you even ask me that?"

A memory of her on her knees just hours earlier sent a wave of heated arousal crashing over him in a red haze. The woman would be the death of him.

Triumph flared in her eyes, and she turned to peer into the frying pan, nodding her approval. "Smart man. Anything I can help with?"

"No, I got this."

She grabbed her laptop and settled on the sofa where she'd been the night before. She sat down in a cross-legged position, and her fingers began flying over the keys. She frowned at the screen several times, then stared blankly off into the distance, as if deep in thought.

CHAPTER EIGHTEEN

~ Aggie ~

T WANTED HER TO GO WITH ZEKE and let things play out, more for appearances' sake than anything else. Refusing to continue would arouse suspicion and inspire questions, which neither of them wanted. Their chosen paths required them to be ghosts.

Or Chameleons.

Thanks to being in the wrong place at the wrong time and getting herself abducted in Parryville, she was going to have to change her colors soon. But knowing T, he already had a plan in mind.

It was no big deal. She'd assumed many identities over the years. The downside was having her time with Zeke come to an end. He'd really grown on her. They had a connection, a natural chemistry, that was hard to come by. Ironically enough, it was their similarities that prevented them from ever seeing one another again. They were both loners. Transients. Unwilling and unable to commit to anyone because of who they were and what they did.

There were exceptions, of course. Aggie knew of at least two of T's operatives who had formed "permanent partnerships," as T called them, but Aggie didn't think anything like that was in her future.

Zeke's, maybe.

Attached with T's coded message was a complete dossier on her current shadow. Zeke really was his name. Zeke Ericsson. He'd served as a SEAL and been considered one of the best until a mission went full-on FUBAR in the Middle East. Men died, highly classified weapons disappeared and wound up in the hands of the enemy, and Zeke walked away with the blame on his shoulders and a dishonorable discharge.

Aggie skimmed the highlights a second time and came to the same conclusion—it didn't add up.

In the first place, no one man at Zeke's level could have been behind a fuckup of that magnitude, not without a lot of inside help and someone much higher up pulling strings. In the second place, if he *had* been a coconspirator, the powers that be wouldn't have let him walk away with nothing more than a badge of shame. They would have charged him with treason and made an example out of him. And in the third place, Zeke was no traitor. She knew that to the depths of her soul.

He was a scapegoat—she was sure of it. The

secret agreement he'd signed was proof of it.

But why had he agreed? Why would an honorable man—a skilled, highly regarded operative—cop to something like that? Who was he protecting?

She glanced over at Zeke, grilling like the sexy boss he was. There was nothing dishonorable about him, except possibly his decision to work for a woman like Charley. He'd said it was the cash, but she wasn't buying it any more than his signed confession that he'd been brokering deals with the enemy.

Just because he spent the day worshipping your body, taking you to heights of ecstasy you'd only imagined before then, doesn't make him a good guy, Aggie.

No, of course it didn't. But she'd thought he was a good guy before the epic sex. And the notes T had included about his service record only strengthened that belief.

His code name was Raguel. The archangel of justice. It fit him as well as Robin Hood fit her.

As if sensing her gaze, Zeke peered at her over his shoulder. "Enjoying the view?" he asked with a smirk.

She was. He was as fine-looking from the back as he was from the front. Broad shoulders and back, adorned with beautiful ink, sporting red marks from her nails, then tapering down into narrow, talented hips. A nice, firm backside, perfect for holding on to while he pistoned between her thighs, currently encased in soft, well-worn denim.

"I'd enjoy it more if you were naked."

He laughed at that, a low, sexy sound. "Grilling naked is asking for trouble."

"Good point," she said on an exhale. "Speaking of, how much longer?"

"Impatient, are we?"

"Hungry," she corrected. "I'm starving."

"You wouldn't be if you ate more than nuts and berries."

She laughed. Her soul just felt lighter with him around.

"I told you, I'm not good in the kitchen."

"Oh, I wouldn't say that," he said, his eyes heating. His gaze slid to the counter. No doubt he was remembering what they'd done there earlier.

"Generally speaking, if I have to cook it, I'm not going to eat it," she continued as if he hadn't spoken.

"Good thing I'm here then. It's just about done."

She closed the lid on her laptop and joined him at the table. The steak was cooked to perfection, as were the vegetables. So much so in fact that she had no problems complimenting him on his culinary skills.

"You are a man of many talents," she told him.

He smiled smugly. "Glad you think so."

"Where'd you learn how to cook like this?"

"I worked in a couple of restaurants as a kid. Picked up a few things."

"Before you went into the service?"

His expression went blank. He grunted and stabbed a thick-cut fry and brought it to his lips.

"Oh, come on. I knew within five minutes of meeting you that you had special training. I doubt you picked it up by watching action-adventure movies."

"Where did you learn your mad hacking skills?"

She shrugged. "Just comes naturally."

He grunted. "That's what I thought."

"Are you still determined to deliver me to Charley?"

His eyes darkened, making her think of the sky right before a storm. "Yes. Nothing has changed."

He was wrong about that. A lot of things had changed. Most notably, her unexpectedly strong temptation to throw caution to the wind and spend the next couple of weeks holed up with him, having great sex and learning more about him.

Perhaps it was for the best. Caring about anything or anyone was a weakness that could be exploited and used against her—or more importantly, against the people she cared about.

Another thing that had changed: she was now privy to information she hadn't had before. Information about him. Information about the woman he was delivering her to. Both presented their share of challenges, but challenges didn't worry her as long as she knew what she was dealing with.

And now that T also knew, she didn't worry at all. If anything happened to her, T would rain hell down from on high.

Aggie pushed back the inconvenient pang of disappointment and kept her expression neutral. "You're right. I should hear what Charley has to say. Should we leave tomorrow morning or head out tonight?"

Zeke narrowed his eyes, suspicious of her easy acceptance, running scenarios in his mind. She knew he was weighing the benefits of staying one more night against the risk that she would slip away.

"The sooner, the better," he said finally. "If we leave tonight, we can be there by midafternoon tomorrow."

She nodded, once again disappointed, but not surprised by his priorities. The mission took precedence.

It's better this way, she told herself. *A swift, clean break.*

Aggie pushed away the remains of her dinner, no longer hungry, and stood. "All right then. Give me fifteen, and I'll be good to go."

His eyes snapped to hers. "I didn't mean we had to leave right this minute."

"No sense in prolonging the inevitable, right?"

she asked, summoning a small, cold smile. "I'm as anxious to get this over with as you are."

She wasn't angry that he intended to complete his mission, because that was the kind of man he was. He did what he said he was going to do—yet another reason why him walking away with a dishonorable discharge didn't ring true.

No, what bothered her was that had their places been reversed, she would have chosen her priorities differently.

* * *

They were on the road within the hour, *borrowing* the Range Rover from the garage. Zeke had been apprehensive about doing so at first because it was a "high-profile ride," but now that she'd made up her mind, she was impatient to close this chapter and move on to the next one.

The ride was quiet, the mood subdued. Gone was that sense of easy acceptance they'd shared for a brief yet wonderful time. Several times, he offered to stop, either to get something to eat or to stretch out the kinks, but she declined.

"The sooner, the better," he'd said, and he was right.

The GPS coordinates Charley had provided led them to a boxy two-story off the beaten path, along a remote stretch of road through a town long forgotten once the newer, faster highways had been built.

A late-model black SUV sat in the driveway, the only indication that they weren't alone.

No sooner had Zeke pulled up to the place than a man stepped out of the front door, donned shades, and walked toward them. Black cargo pants. Black polo. Clean-cut. Utterly expressionless.

"I guess this is it," she said quietly.

Zeke nodded, eyeing the man's approach as if he was suddenly having second thoughts.

Too late for that, she thought, opening the passenger door.

"I'll see you inside," Zeke offered, reaching for his own door.

"Don't bother. Your mission's complete."

He frowned at that.

"You know, the Rover suits you. You should keep it."

The man who approached the car pulled her door open further, then tossed a thick envelope onto the seat she'd just vacated, and said, "The final installment."

The sound of the door closing resonated through her, more significant than the simple closing of a vehicle door should have sounded.

"If you'll come with me, please," the agent said.

"Lead the way."

Aggie straightened her spine, lifted her chin, and walked into the house behind him. She was proud of herself. She didn't look back once.

CHAPTER NINETEEN

~ Zeke ~

ZEKE WATCHED AS AGGIE MOVED away from him. Her head was held high, her body language relaxed, as if she were heading in for coffee with friends. She didn't look back once. His chest tightened and squeezed, building to a painful crescendo when the door closed behind her.

His hand was still on the handle. He got the door open a scant six inches before it was forcibly closed by a second man who'd appeared out of nowhere, dressed almost identically to the first—a study in black SWAT gear. Same close-cropped hair, blank expression, and fucking mirrored aviators.

"My instructions are to deliver her to Charley," Zeke said, which wasn't entirely true. When he'd called the night before to give Charley an approximate ETA, she'd thanked him and told him he would receive final payment upon safe delivery of the package. She never actually said she'd be there personally to accept.

"Charley is awaiting her arrival at a secure location."

Zeke frowned. "Charley's not here? Perhaps I should accompany her—"

"She's no longer your concern, Mr. Ericsson."

The guy shifted slightly, just enough to let Zeke know he was heavily armed. When Zeke made no move to leave, another man appeared. Then another. Zeke looked around, then spotted the glint of metal aimed his way from a sniper on the roof about the same time a tiny red dot appeared on his chest.

What the fuck did I just do?

Aloud, he said, "Right."

"Phone, please."

The guy standing just outside the open car window held out his hand. Zeke reluctantly put the shiny black burner into it.

"And the picture."

"Long gone," Zeke lied.

The guy stared at him through his mirrored shades for several long moments, then gave a single head nod to his colleagues and stepped back.

Zeke shifted into reverse and backed out of the drive, heading back toward the main road. The flat plains stretched out beyond the town, making it impossible for him to pull off without being seen, and he had no doubt he was being watched.

His chest tightened again, and he rubbed at it absently. What was his problem? He'd known this was how it would end. He'd been hired to do a job, and he'd done it. He had money in his pocket and was once again free to go wherever and do whatever he wanted.

He drove until he came to the next town, then pulled into a roadside gas station. He picked up the envelope and peered inside. Bundles of cash, more than double what he'd already been paid up to that point. Enough to cover his expenses for the next couple of years, more if he was careful.

It made the weight on his chest even heavier.

He filled up the tank, emptied his own, and got back in the Rover.

"Fuck it," he said to no one in particular. Instead of continuing on, he went back the way he'd come.

The black sedan wasn't in the driveway. He knew before he even got out of the Rover that he was too late. The place was empty, and Aggie was gone.

He went inside anyway and gave the place a thorough once-over. There was no indication that anyone had stepped foot in the house in the last twenty years, and no clue where they might have gone.

Zeke raked his hand down his face and stood in the center of the living room.

"FUCK!" he shouted into the empty space around him.

CHAPTER TWENTY

~ *Aggie* ~

After Aggie entered the house, she was led to the back and told to wait. Her escort appeared to be listening to something via an earpiece. He wasn't as personable as Zeke, nor as easy on the eyes. He was all business, almost robotic in his speech and mannerisms. Given the choice, she preferred Zeke's long hair, tattoos, and slightly rough around the edges manner.

Within minutes, her escort signaled to another guy who had come in behind them, and they ushered Aggie out the back to a waiting SUV, identical to the one that had been out front. She glanced toward the driveway as they circled around toward the road. The Rover was gone. Apparently, Zeke had gotten over whatever second thoughts he might have been having. For a few minutes there, she could have sworn he hadn't wanted to let her go.

It was just more wishful thinking on her part, nothing but romantic notions she'd wrapped around a man who had seen her as a job. A job with *benefits*.

Of course, she'd benefitted, too. The sex had been fantastic. If it hadn't meant as much to him, well, there wasn't anything she could do about that.

Regardless, it didn't matter. Whatever had been between them—real or imagined—was over. Zeke had his cash and could cross her off his to-do list. Aggie took a deep breath, pushed Zeke out of her mind, and focused on her upcoming meeting with the enigmatic Charley.

Other than terse but polite commands, no one spoke to her. They drove for a short time, arriving at an unremarkable airfield, where she was shuttled aboard a waiting helicopter. Once seated, she was blindfolded and fitted with noise-canceling earphones.

It wasn't the first time she'd been in a chopper, but it was the first time she'd done so without the ability to see or hear. The sensation in her belly was exaggerated, exhilarating and terrifying at the same time.

The flight was relatively short, no more than an hour or two, and before she knew it, they landed in a field. The air was crisp and clean. The ache in her head and overall sense of dizziness suggested a higher altitude than she was used to.

Only once she was led into a building and seated were the blindfold and headphones removed. She blinked rapidly in the low-level light and tried to concentrate on her surroundings instead of the nausea.

No windows. One door. A conference table with a tray containing a thermal carafe and a glass. Two padded ergonomic chairs. Nothing else.

The woman who entered the room was tall and slim, with white-blonde hair and pale skin, and well-dressed in a conservative but expensive feminine power suit. She had an air of importance about her; her movements were crisp and efficient.

She poured water from the carafe into the glass and held it out to Aggie. "Here. This will help."

Aggie accepted the glass and sipped. The cool water tasted delicious, as if it had come directly from a mountain spring. She didn't worry about being drugged or anything along those lines. It didn't make sense to drug her now.

"Charley, I presume?"

The woman smiled but didn't confirm. "I apologize for the secrecy."

"No need. You've gone to a lot of trouble to bring me here. I'd like to know why."

Charley nodded, approval shining in her eyes. "Direct and to the point. I like that. Unfortunately, I can't give you the answers you're looking for. You weren't even on our radar until a few weeks ago. Now that you are, I'm rather intrigued myself."

"I don't understand. Who are you? And what changed?"

Charley cocked her head. "I work for a shadow

organization, one that prefers to remain innominate. We assist in a variety of delicate situations, including but not limited to, civilian asset extractions from potentially harmful situations."

"My abduction," Aggie mused.

Charley nodded. "We received word of your situation, as well as a rather convincing case for why we should care. You have some very powerful guardian angels looking out for you, Robin Hood."

Considering so few people knew what she did, Aggie had a sneaking suspicion she knew who one of those powerful guardian angels was. She sat back and sipped more water. "Okay. I'm safe. What now?"

"My instructions were clear. I'm to put you on a private jet, where you will be flown to an undisclosed location of your choice."

"That's it?"

"That's it."

"You're not going to at least try to convince me to work for you?"

Charley laughed softly. "Of course, I am. We could use someone with your skills, and we do have several hours before I put you on that plane. I understand you work alone, but I think you'd do well here. We like to think of ourselves as equalizers. We level the playing field, so to speak. Much like you with your ... charity work."

Aggie nodded and grinned. Secret organizations had their place and served their purpose, but Aggie preferred self-employment. That didn't mean she didn't want to know more about Charley's organization. One never knew when that kind of knowledge could come in handy.

Aloud, she said, "Fair enough. I'm listening. Give me your best recruitment pitch."

CHAPTER TWENTY-ONE

~ Zeke ~

ZEKE WAS A DAMN GOOD TRACKER, but he'd hit a dead end.

Aggie was gone, and he'd probably never see her again.

He returned to his motel room and tried to let it go. Finding Aggie—correction, finding Robin Hood—had been a task, and he'd completed it. It was over. It was time to let it go and move on.

Except he couldn't, for the same reasons he'd taken the job in the first place. Her eyes. They kept appearing behind his lids every time he closed them, beckoning, beseeching. The harder he tried to ignore it, the more determined his brain was to not let him.

Everything reminded him of her. When he looked at the bed, he saw her sitting cross-legged atop the covers, either meditating or staring at the screen of her laptop, absently chewing her lip. When he got food, he thought of her penchant for healthy stuff. He couldn't look at a shower curtain without imagining her peeking out at him, irritated and looking like the most adorable wet baby raccoon.

He'd imagined then what it would be like to touch that skin, to find out if it was as soft as it looked. Now, he knew that it was.

He knew a lot of other things too. Like beneath that nerdy exterior was a woman with great passion in her soul.

And not just passionate. She was intelligent and cunning, too. A wanderer, like him. And versatile. She was as comfortable in a multimillion-dollar dream house as she was a cheap motel room.

The thought made him pause. He imagined her sitting in the chalet, as if she owned the place.

Her words echoed in his head. *"Who says I'm squatting? Maybe this is my place."*

He remembered the amusement in her eyes when she'd said that, how they'd sparkled, as if she was daring him to believe her.

He hadn't.

"The Rover suits you. You should keep it."

"I've never lied to you, Zeke."

What if she'd been telling him the truth all along?

He started to remember other things too. Things he'd thought were incongruent at the time, but he'd passed them off as unimportant. The organic stuff in her fridge. The slick tech. People earning minimum wage under the table didn't have that stuff. Nor did they typically practice meditation or know what Cebuano was.

Then, there was her philanthropy. Paupers weren't typically philanthropic. It defied basic human nature. Sure, there were people who wanted to help others, but only after they took care of themselves.

He was a perfect example. He took care of himself first. Granted, he was a man of simple means. He'd grown up poor. Joined the Navy, so he'd have a roof over his head and food in his belly. Now that he was out, he hadn't changed much. He did what he had to do to get by, using his skills to ensure his basic needs were met, whether that be working per diem in a tattoo shop or hiring himself out as a mercenary.

The point was, everything he did these days, he did for himself. But Aggie? She could wrap herself in wealth anytime she wanted to, but she didn't.

Things clicked into place, like tumblers in a combination lock.

Robin Hood.

Legend had it that Robin Hood was of noble birth. Maybe Aggie was too. Maybe it was about more than redistributing funds. Perhaps Aggie, like Robin Hood, had left her castle and wealthy, powerful family and lived amongst the poor common folk, fighting with them and for them.

If that was the case, then there was a whole lot more to the woman than he'd ever imagined.

Fuck.

Why hadn't he seen it before? She was a master at assuming identities. Why wouldn't she have done so with him too?

Except she had shown him some of her true self, hadn't she?

No longer worried about ditching the Rover, he drove back to the chalet. It was empty and ... clean. Too clean. The place smelled of lemons. Since they'd left, the linens had been replaced, the used towels had been removed, and the garbage had been taken out along with any perishable food items.

He went through the place, top to bottom, and found nothing. No clue to her real identity.

But someone knew. There had to be property records. Utility accounts. Vehicle registrations.

He was a tracker, goddamn it. He'd find her. And this time, he wasn't working for anyone, except himself.

CHAPTER TWENTY-TWO

~ *Aggie* ~

"SHE OFFERED YOU A JOB, DIDN'T SHE?" T asked, leaning back in the deck chair, lifting his already-tanned face to the tropical sun.

After leaving Charley, Aggie had taken the jet to LA and vanished. She'd liked Charley well enough, but she trusted no one—especially not someone in Charley's position. Now that Charley knew she existed, Aggie was going to have to rethink how she went about doing things.

So she'd decided to go off grid for a while. To take a break and regroup. There was no place better to do that than her private island, and no one better to provide answers than her brother. Only one person had the connections and knowledge to pull a stunt like that, and he was currently sitting right beside her.

"She had a hell of a sales pitch," Aggie admitted.

"You're not interested?"

"In working for her? No. Too many rules."

T chuckled softly. As a former SEAL, he knew all about rules and didn't care for them any more than she did. That was why he'd created his own organization. To be a Chameleon, the rules were few and simple: cut all ties and cease to exist.

Unlike Charley, however, he didn't only recruit already-trained operatives who'd proven themselves. He took regular people, those who had nothing and no one and gave them everything—training, purpose, a chance to exact vengeance.

Not everyone could be a Chameleon though. T hand-selected his people. Each was carefully screened and thoroughly researched. He said he knew within minutes of talking with a potential candidate whether they had what it took. He hadn't been wrong yet. In fact, many of his operatives believed he was psychic—a rumor which T did nothing to discourage.

"Plus, you know I can't stand the idea of answering to anyone," she added, almost as an afterthought.

"You answer to me."

She laughed. "You wish."

"I do wish," he said on a sigh. "I wouldn't have to call in markers to get your butt out of trouble quite as often."

She shielded her eyes and glared at him. "Excuse me?"

"You heard me. You're brilliant, but you're not good in the field."

"I'm good in the field," she protested.

"You were *abducted*. You got *hurt*. And it's not the first time."

Well, there was that. "That wasn't my fault."

"You got sloppy."

She clamped her lips together and said nothing because he was right. She hadn't seen the threat until it was too late.

Aggie knew her greatest value was in her digital skills. However, she couldn't stand the thought of sitting behind a screen day in and day out. It was too confining. Too restrictive. She needed to move. To live in the real world and be with real people. T understood that, even if he'd prefer that she'd stay safe and work from within a luxurious ivory tower.

"Has there been any word on Sam?"

"Still MIA."

"Someone should do something."

"Such as?"

"Find Sam and figure out what's on those files. I get why he'd run from the mob guys, but from the FBI? Something stinks about that whole situation, and it's not just the pollution in Parryville."

"Hmm," T hummed noncommittally. "Tracking. Obtaining information. Meting out justice. Sounds like exactly the kind of thing a certain mercenary specializes in. For a price, of course."

Zeke.

Just the name was enough to make her body respond. Not a day had gone by when she hadn't thought about him or that last full day they'd spent together at the chalet.

Or the way he dropped her off at the safe house, taken his cash, and skedaddled.

A soft breeze blew over them from the water, only slightly cooler than the air. Aggie turned over, letting the sun warm her back—partly to even out her tan and partly to avoid T's assessing gaze. The man saw everything. His code name wasn't Taser for nothing.

"Maybe someone should hire him to do it," T continued.

"I thought *you* wanted to hire him," Aggie said, remembering the way T's eyes had lit up in interest.

"No."

"How come? Didn't he live up to your expectations?"

"Oh, he's done that and more. The guy's good. He tracked you all the way to Mount Elbert."

"How the hell did he do that?" she asked, astonished.

"I told you, he's the best. By the time he got there though, Charley was gone, and the facility went back to being a sad casualty of the post–Cold War era."

"So … if he's that good, what's the problem?"

"You are."

"Excuse me?"

"I can't have another besotted agent. People are going to start thinking I have a heart, and that's bad for business."

Her heart swelled in her chest. "Besotted, huh?" Then, she remembered their last day together and shook her head. "No, he was only too glad to be rid of me."

"Well, he blew through more than fifty grand in a matter of weeks, looking for you. That says something, don't you think?"

Her heart leaped, though she was afraid to hope. Afraid to believe that the regret she'd seen in his eyes when she got out of that vehicle wasn't just her imagination.

Aggie extended an arm and ran her fingers through the pristine white sand. The sun beat down on her back. The waves lapped gently at the shore just yards from where they lounged.

What would Zeke think of this place? Did he even like the beach? Was he more of a mountain guy?

Finally, she said, "He didn't do what the Navy said he did, did he?"

"No, he didn't," T confirmed.

"So, why'd he sign the papers that said he did?"

"That's the question, isn't it?" T mused, though she had a feeling he already knew. "You can ask him when you hire him."

She snorted. "I have no idea where he is or how to get in touch with him."

"Good thing I do then."

Her hand lifted from the sand and shot out to the side. She grabbed a bit of the soft skin at the back of his arm between her thumb and index finger and twisted. Hard.

"*Timothy.*"

"Ow!" he exclaimed, brushing her hand away. "What was that for?"

"You know where he is?"

"Of course I do. What kind of big brother would I be if I didn't?"

CHAPTER TWENTY-THREE

~ *Zeke* ~

As a base of operations, the chalet was pretty sweet. Isolation. State-of-the-art conveniences. Spectacular view.

That level of luxury had never been a part of his life, so it took some getting used to. Now that he'd become accustomed to it, it would be harder to return to a drifter-type lifestyle that required staying in fleabag rat traps, picking up work and meals where he could.

He wondered how Aggie managed to move so effortlessly between worlds. Or why she would want to if she had a place like this.

The upscale living was one more thing to secretly crave, right along with a sense of purpose, being part of a team, and Aggie Mays—or whatever she was calling herself these days.

Still, he wouldn't have stayed there if he hadn't thought it was his best chance of crossing paths with her again. He had hoped that after meeting with Charley, she would return to the chalet.

It was true what they said: *You can't miss what you never had. But once you had it…*

Aggie was right there at the top of his list. He hadn't known what had been missing from his life, but now it was painfully obvious. Her.

Nearly six weeks later, she remained in the breeze, and he was no closer to finding her.

That didn't mean he'd stopped looking. He used everything he'd learned about her—her habits, her patterns, her preferences—to try to locate her. He researched and cross-referenced. He'd blown through the cash he'd earned from Charley, following up leads, paying for information.

The woman was a fucking ghost.

And far more than he'd ever given her credit for.

He was pondering that one night on the balcony, staring out at the scenic view with a glass of quality liquor in his hand. The sun set behind the mountains in a spectacular display. The sky turned deep midnight blue, holding more stars than he'd ever seen in his life.

It was stunning, and yet he felt the restlessness starting to stir. The waiting was getting to him. He wanted to be out, doing something.

"Nice night, huh?"

The familiar voice was a smooth stroke over his skin. He spun around, afraid his eyes were playing tricks on him.

"Aggie!"

"I heard you might be looking for me."

Without conscious thought, he closed the space between them and drew her into his arms. He lowered his head and pressed his lips to hers, unleashing the last six weeks of worry, frustration, and regret into the kiss. She took it all.

When he pulled away, he laid his forehead against hers. "You came back. You're okay."

"I came back. I'm okay."

"Listen, I'm sorry. I shouldn't have—"

"No, you listen," she said, putting a finger to his lips. "No talking tonight, okay?"

"No talking?"

"No talking."

"What shall we do then?"

Her hand stroked his chest, causing shivers to travel down his spine. The woman's touch did things to him. Wiped thoughts of everything but getting her naked and moaning his name in ecstasy from his mind.

He palmed her ass and lifted, pleased when she wrapped her arms around his neck and her legs around his hips. Lowering his mouth, he kissed her like a man possessed because that was exactly what he was.

She opened for him eagerly, welcoming his tongue while her nails scraped against the back of his scalp and she pulled at his hair. He thought about taking her inside, then decided against it. He backed her up against the glass and used the pressure to hold her in place while he made quick work of pulling down her stretchy leggings.

He set her on her feet only long enough to allow her to kick them off while he released and wrapped himself. Within the span of a few heartbeats, she was back in his arms, up against the glass, and he was sliding inside her. She was so hot. So wet. So ready. She moaned in pleasure, and he felt it everywhere.

Her tight sheath squeezed around him, drawing him in deeper, even as her arms and legs did the same. When he bottomed out, he paused, giving them both a moment. She needed to adjust to his intrusion. He needed to rein in the animalistic urge to fuck until they both saw stars.

It was even better than he remembered. Absolute bliss.

He began to move, her rhythmic clenching suggesting she was already close. He was right there with her. He pulled his hips back in a long, reluctant withdrawal until nothing remained inside her, except the tip. Then he pushed forward with a sudden, powerful thrust, burying himself so deep that it was impossible to tell where he left off and she began.

"Again," she whispered huskily.

He was only too glad to oblige. Repeatedly.

"*Zeke.*"

His name on her lips was a desperate plea. She was looking up at him, her eyes filled with want and need and so much more—a mirror image of everything inside him. He held her gaze and buried himself deep in her body, feeling her climax almost as intensely as he felt his own.

They stayed like that, clinging to one another, hearts pounding, breaths heavy, staring into each other's eyes.

Deep in his chest, something shifted, and he knew nothing would ever be the same.

* * *

He stroked a finger down the curve of her back, savoring the smooth silkiness of her skin and the sense of deja vu. Daylight streamed in through the window, revealing the dips and curves he'd been worshipping through the night. Her skin was lightly bronzed, as if she'd spent some time in the sun since the last time he'd seen her. The golden highlights streaking her rich brown hair further corroborated his theory.

"That feels good," she murmured in the sated purr of a satisfied woman.

The sex had been wild and desperate at first, but as the night wore on, it had become slower, less physical, more emotional. It was new territory for him, but he wasn't panicking like he probably should have been. He'd already accepted that this woman had gotten under his skin. Now, he just had to figure out what to do about it.

Where had she gone, and why? Did she have other hideaways like this around the country? Around the globe? Other men who had become as obsessed with her as he had?

He had so many questions. What he went with first was, "Who *are* you?"

She turned over and graced him with a smile before she touched her lips to his. "The woman whose world you rocked last night."

It wasn't the answer he wanted, but it would do for now. "You did some rocking of your own."

Her smile widened. "What can I say? I missed you."

"I was looking for you."

"I know. That's why I came."

"What took you so long?"

"I was … away. I didn't know you were here until recently."

Away where? With whom? He clamped those questions down before they made it over his lips and said instead, "I thought you might have been angry with me for delivering you to Charley."

"More disappointed than angry, but I get it."

"You do?"

"Yes. You're a man of your word. You told me your intentions up front and never wavered. I respect that even if I didn't like it."

"What happened?"

"Nothing much, honestly. We talked. I walked. It was all very anticlimactic."

"And now?"

"Now, I'm ready to take care of unfinished business."

"What unfinished business?" he asked, narrowing his eyes and wondering if *he* was the unfinished business.

"I want to go back to Parryville and get some answers, and I want you to help me."

"Me? Why me?"

"Because you're the best. And you offered, remember?"

His lips curled wryly at the memory of that conversation. "If I recall, you said you couldn't afford my help."

"That was before."

"Before what?"

"Before you spent six weeks and fifty thousand dollars trying to find me. Why did you do that, Zeke?" she asked softly. "Why didn't you just take the money and go?"

His jaw tightened. He didn't have a good answer for that, at least not one he was willing to speak aloud. "I don't know."

"Admit it. I grew on you, didn't I?"

He grunted. Her eyes glittered.

"Ah, I missed that sound. Come on. I need coffee and probably a shower."

He wasn't opposed to either of those things. "Coffee's on you. I haven't been able to figure out how to use that damn machine."

"I'll show you. That way, you can bring me coffee and breakfast in bed tomorrow morning."

"Who says I'm going to be here in the morning?" he grumbled. Of course he was going to be there in the morning. He was going to be wherever she was until he figured out whatever this was between them.

She laughed. The sound was like a balm to his soul. He pushed aside the doubts and decided to live in the moment.

The lesson in expensive coffee machine operation took a while. He kept getting distracted, and when he did, he distracted her as well. She didn't seem to mind.

"So, what's your deal?" Zeke asked later, once they'd managed to make coffee, take a shower, and sit down to breakfast. "How does a socially conscious hacker who rents condemned apartments and works in bars afford a place like this?"

"Who says it's mine?"

"Isn't it?"

She smiled serenely and sipped her coffee. Instead of answering, she asked a question of her own. "Why is a highly skilled former special operative drifting across the country, working as a tattooist and moonlighting as a mercenary?"

When he said nothing, she said, "I guess we both have our secrets, don't we?"

Well, she had him there.

"Tell me why you want to go back to

Parryville."

"I wasn't the only one looking into the paper mill's illegal activities. Apparently, the FBI was too. Same general topic—illegal toxic dumping—but from a different angle. They were investigating allegations of ties to organized crime, particularly in the area of waste disposal."

It seemed like one hell of a coincidence that the FBI just happened to be in Parryville at the same time as the elusive Robin Hood, but that was him. He didn't believe in coincidences, and he sure as hell didn't trust the feds.

Aggie continued. "A second-shift supervisor by the name of Sam Higgins was tapped as an informant to aid in the investigation, but something went wrong. Sam disappeared the night I was abducted."

He frowned. "You think your abduction had something to do with that?"

"It doesn't make sense otherwise. If the FBI was working with Sam and keeping an eye on him, then they know the last time Sam was seen was when he walked me home that night."

An uncomfortable feeling tightened his chest. "You and Higgins. You had a thing?"

He tried to keep his voice level, so he didn't sound like a jealous, possessive asshole. Judging by the way her eyes flashed, he hadn't pulled it off.

"No. We went out a few times, but it was nothing serious. I was very clear that I wasn't looking for anything other than a friend."

Zeke snorted. "Yeah? What was *he* looking for?"

She smiled, as if his reaction pleased her. "Sometimes, he came into the bar after his shift, looking like he carried the world on his shoulders. I lent a sympathetic—and somewhat opportunistic—ear."

"He gave you inside intel on what was going on at the mill," he guessed.

She nodded. "Unintentionally, yes."

It was as if a lightbulb had gone on in his head. He'd been racking his brain, trying to figure out why a woman who could afford a place like this would choose to continually reinvent herself and live like a pauper.

"That's why you do it. The shitty apartments, the minimum wage jobs. For the inside intel."

"In part," she agreed. "Online research can get me pretty far, but it doesn't always tell the whole story. Only people can do that. The people who are involved, and the people who are affected."

"In part, you said. What's the rest of it?"

"Restless person syndrome," she said with a slight curl of her lips. "This chalet is my anchor. My home base, if you will. But I can't stay here for more than a couple of weeks without feeling suffocated. I can't be just one person, doing just one thing day in and day out. I need to travel to different places, and have new experiences."

That was something he understood completely. "You have a nomadic soul."

"Nomadic soul. I like that. It sounds better than RPS."

Did her "anchor" analogy include people she returned to or just places? Again, he wondered where she'd been and who she'd been with. It was on the tip of his tongue to ask, but he refrained. He wasn't sure he wanted to know the answer. She was asking him to return to Parryville with her and tie off some loose ends. That would have to be enough—for now.

"All right, you've got yourself a mercenary."

"Excellent."

Her smile lit off a series of fireworks in his chest.

"When do you want to leave?"

"Tomorrow, after you bring me coffee and breakfast in bed."

He stood and walked around to her side of the breakfast bar. He remained standing, leaned back against the granite so that he faced her, and crossed his arms. "Shouldn't we discuss my fee?"

Her gaze lowered from his eyes and worked its way downward slowly, then back up again. It was like a blatant stroke to his cock, and his cock responded accordingly. She pushed back from the counter and tugged her robe open.

"Yes, let's."

CHAPTER TWENTY-FOUR

~ *Aggie* ~

ADMITTEDLY, HIS PRICE WAS STEEP. Had any other man suggested such a fee, she wouldn't have considered it. But he wasn't any other man. He was Zeke, the white knight mercenary and kindred soul who knew how to make her body melt and her blood sing.

"So, what's the plan?" he asked as he rubbed the towel over his wet hair.

Fresh from the shower, he wore loose sweats low on his slim hips. She took a moment to admire the view, then shook her head to clear it and focus.

"We go back to Parryville, find Sam, get him to tell us what he knows, then exact some vengeance."

He smirked. "Exact vengeance?"

"Yes," she replied firmly. "I don't appreciate being thrown under the bus, and I *really* don't appreciate being roughed up."

His eyes practically glowed at the reminder as they scanned her body, pausing on those areas that had sustained the most damage. His look was possessive. Intense. In that moment, she understood why his code name was Raguel. He looked exactly like a beautiful, fierce archangel, ready to rain down justice on those who'd hurt her. In that moment, she'd never felt more cherished.

She pulled out her laptop and connected to the secure cache of information she'd compiled on Parryville. There were more files there than there had been. Since her brother was the only other person on earth with access to the information, they must have come from him despite his assertion that Sam Higgins and the Parryville situation weren't on his "playground."

Zeke sat down beside her on the massive sectional, bringing with him the scents of soap, shaving cream, and something uniquely him.

She turned her screen, so he could see it. "This is what I've got so far. Read through it and tell me what you think we'll need."

He accepted the laptop and began to read while she took her turn in the bathroom. They'd agreed that showering separately was more conducive to getting things done than showering together. When they were naked around each other, they had trouble concentrating on anything else.

It was odd, this obsession developing between them. They couldn't get enough of one another. She'd never experienced anything like it before. Aggie wasn't complaining, however. As a devout practitioner of mindfulness and living in the moment, she was going to enjoy it while she could. Nothing this powerful, this intense, could last. She just had to keep that in the back of her mind every time her heart tried to suggest otherwise.

Zeke was where she'd left him when she emerged. He glanced up at her briefly, his expression unreadable, then went back to reading. There was a lot of information to wade through. It included her notes based on conversations with Sam, detailed schedules of disposal and route schematics, a list of paper mill employees involved in the process and an in-depth financial analysis on each one, as well as dossiers on the FBI task force and the organized crime situation in the area.

She made a cup of herbal tea, then went out onto the balcony to meditate. If they were going to do this, she would need to be in the proper headspace.

She sat cross-legged on a soft cushion, closed her eyes, and began with some deep breathing exercises. Her body was already loose and relaxed. She lifted her face to the sky and opened her heart, allowing herself to drift away.

When she opened her eyes again, Zeke was sitting on the balcony with her. It was a testament to how safe she felt in his presence that she could lose herself so thoroughly.

"All finished?" she asked.

"All finished," he confirmed. "You're fucking amazing, you know that?"

Very few people knew she existed, let alone what she did, and that was okay. She wasn't in it for accolades or recognition. Quite the opposite in fact. But hearing those words from Zeke, a man who did his own share of work from the shadows, warmed her from the inside out.

"Glad you think so."

"I do." He waved his hand in her general direction. "Does that help?"

"Meditation?"

He nodded.

"Yes. It's great for clearing the mind and improving focus. Have you ever tried it?"

"No. Tattooing does that for me. I lose myself in it. The hum of the machine. Taking feelings and memories and turning them into art that means something. Not the bangers," he clarified. "Not the premade designs that everyone gets, but the ones that come from the soul. Those that honor a loved one or turn intangible beliefs into something that can be seen and touched."

"That's beautiful," she said softly.

She rose from the ground and straddled his lap. His hands rested lightly on her hips while she ran her fingers over his chest and arms. Such intricate designs, all different and yet in perfect harmony.

"Do all of your tattoos mean something to you?"

"Most of them do. Some I got when I was young and stupid."

"What about this one?" She pressed the pads of her fingers to one of the larger images, a complex piece that covered his shoulder, extending down his arm and onto his chest. It incorporated animals—a wolf and a raven—around what looked like an ancient compass, etched with runes and surrounded by symbols. "It looks Nordic."

"It is," he confirmed. "A nod to my Viking ancestry."

She trailed her finger farther down his torso, then across to his arm and the frog skeleton hidden among more symbols. "And this. I've seen this before. It's a bone frog, isn't it? You're a Navy SEAL."

He gently grabbed her hand and lifted it to his lips. "Yes, it's a bone frog. And, no, I'm not a SEAL. Not anymore."

His tone warned her not to ask any more questions. She didn't. Instead, she leaned her upper body against his and rested her head in the crook of his neck in a gesture of acceptance. He wrapped his arms around her and held her close, and she knew he'd gotten the message.

She pressed a kiss to his lips and changed the subject.

"Do you think Sam's still alive?"

"Yes, I think he's alive," Zeke replied after considering her question. "Alive and hiding in the mountains. He grew up around there, right? He's an avid hunter and fisherman. Those skills and his knowledge of the area are to his advantage, but they won't last forever. I'm more concerned with why he ran. Based on his behavior and the things he said, he knew he was in danger. If he was an informant, why wouldn't the FBI protect him?"

"Maybe he didn't think they could. Or maybe it was the FBI he was afraid of," she offered, thinking of what had happened to the Boston bank president.

He didn't immediately discount the possibility. "A dirty agent?"

Aggie shrugged. "It's possible. It wouldn't be the first time someone abused their position to line their own pockets."

"No," Zeke agreed darkly. "It certainly wouldn't."

CHAPTER TWENTY-FIVE

~ *Aggie* ~

THEY LEFT THE NEXT MORNING under mostly cloudy skies and the threat of rain. Typically, she felt mentally prepared and eager to be embarking on a new adventure. This time, however, uncertainty hovered around the edges of their departure from the chalet. She wasn't going alone. She had to consider someone else in her decisions, which was both comforting and worrisome.

She'd booked them flights—under assumed names and with professional-quality fake IDs, of course—to cover the bulk of the distance as quickly as possible, then procured a vehicle to take them the rest of the way.

"Why are we heading north?" he asked when Aggie directed him toward the interstate turnoff.

"You said a real-time, detailed satellite map of the mountains around Parryville would be helpful."

"Yes. So?"

"So, we're going to get one." When he opened

his mouth to protest, she said, "Trust me, okay?"

He didn't look happy about it, but he nodded. They drove through lush farmlands amid rolling hills, working their way up into the mountains of Pennsylvania to a town called Pine Ridge. He looked really confused when she directed him to a local garage there.

"What are we doing here?"

"Trust me."

He grunted and exhaled, not entirely pleased with the situation but willing to give her the benefit of the doubt.

Aggie got out of the rental and walked toward one of the open bays, where a large, muscular man with close-cropped black hair worked on a classic Chevelle. He looked up and tracked her approach.

Aggie heard the car door close behind her and knew that Zeke had spotted the guy, too, and decided to follow. The guy working on the Chevelle straightened slowly, assessing them both with the skill and experience of the operative he was.

She'd heard so much about Sean Callaghan from her brother. Mostly complaints. Though T respected the hell out of his former SEAL teammate, Sean was the one who had "compromised"—T's word, not hers—one of his best agents.

"Can I help you?"

"I hope so. I'm looking for Nix."

Outwardly, the man didn't change, but the air

around them seemed to cool about twenty degrees. His eyes went to Zeke, then back to her.

"Sorry, can't help you."

Rather than be deterred, she smiled. "Yeah, Taser said you'd say that."

Sean's intense blue eyes narrowed. "Taser? Is that supposed to mean something to me?"

Aggie continued as if he hadn't spoken. "Taser also said if you did say that, I should respond with, *Honduras*."

His eyes widened almost imperceptibly.

"Sean, what's going on?"

A woman came out from the bay and went up to the man's side, slipping her hand into his back pocket. She was a little older than she had been the last time Aggie saw her, but she was still beautifully striking. Long jet-black hair. Lithe and toned. But it was her eyes, nearly colorless, like diamonds, that Aggie remembered most.

"Robin?" Nicki Callaghan—known to Aggie by her Chameleon name, Nix—said. "Is that really you?"

"Hey, Nix. Been a while, huh?"

"I'll say! What are you doing here?"

"We could use some help."

Aggie felt Zeke shift beside her, momentarily drawing Nix's attention. Nix took in his hair, his piercings, his visible tatts, and then she looked back to Aggie and raised an eyebrow.

"He's with you?"

"He is."

"I approve," Nix murmured. "Come on in. Let's talk." She looked back to Zeke. "You, stay here. Sean, baby, why don't you take him down to the pub while Robin and I have a chat, will you?"

Without waiting for an answer, Nix turned and walked around the side of the garage.

Zeke reached out and touched her arm. "What the hell?"

"Go have a beer with Sean, okay? I got this."

"I don't think so."

"Look, I know you have questions, but you're just going to have to trust me." Neither her brother's nor Nix's secrets were hers to share.

"I don't like this."

"I know, and I'm sorry. But I'm asking you to trust me. Please."

It was the third time she'd made that request since they'd arrived, and hopefully, it would be the last. There was only so much blind faith she could ask of him.

He studied her face, looking deep into her eyes, then nodded reluctantly.

"Thank you," she whispered.

Aggie left an unhappy-looking Zeke with Sean and followed Nix into the spacious living quarters above the garage.

"All right, first things first," Nix said. "Who's the stud?"

"His name's Zeke. He's helping me out with

something."

Nix's eyebrow rose again. "I thought you worked alone."

"I do, usually, but I made an exception in this case. I mean, look at him. Pretty hot, right?" Aggie grinned mischievously.

"He is," Nix agreed. "But he's got badass written all over him."

"Like your husband doesn't."

"Fair point." Nix's eyes widened. "Wait. This is about more than a mission, isn't it? You really *like* this guy."

Aggie shrugged. "He's got skills."

"Skills, huh? So ... you're *not* that into him?"

"Fine! Just the opposite, okay? I'm *too* into him. The only time I feel whole is when I'm with him. That's crazy, right? I mean, I've only known him for a short while and what we have ... it's so intense. So powerful. So ..." Aggie clamped her lips together, shocked by her sudden and uncharacteristic bout of word vomit, but damn it, Nix was the closest thing to a friend she had.

"Unsustainable?" Nix finished.

"Yes! Exactly."

Nix's lips curled. "Maybe he's your *croie*."

"My what?"

"Your soul mate. Your perfect match."

Aggie started shaking her head, but Nix wasn't finished. "I know. It seems impossible, but everything you described sounds exactly like the way I felt when I met Sean. And let me tell you, if he is your *croie*, then that connection you're feeling will not only endure, but it'll grow even stronger over time."

"I'm not sure I can handle anything stronger," Aggie admitted.

"You can handle a lot more than you think you can, especially when you don't have to do it alone. Now, tell me what you need."

Aggie gave her a brief rundown of the Parryville situation as well as what she hoped to accomplish.

"A live, detailed satellite feed. That's all you want?"

"For now."

"Shouldn't be a problem. It might take a bit to get it into optimal position though."

"How much time?"

"Depends. A satellite can orbit the earth in ninety minutes, but it might be otherwise engaged. I'd say no more than twenty-four hours on the outside."

Aggie had expected as much. "Can you send me a link?"

"*That* might be a problem," Nix admitted, tapping her finger against her lip. "These guys, they're very protective of their toys, especially private satellites that technically don't exist. I might have a solution though. Let me make a few calls."

"Thanks. I really appreciate it."

"Anything for you."

Nix moved into the other room and spoke quietly into her phone. Aggie took the time to look around, smiling when she saw the wall of pictures. It was strange, seeing a Chameleon actually living a semi-normal life.

There were lots of photos of men with dark hair and blue eyes, many of similar size and features, plus wives and kids. Aggie recognized Nix's husband in many of them but had to blink when she saw a few where he seemed to be standing next to himself.

"No, you're not seeing double. That's Sean's twin," Nix told her, coming to stand beside her.

"Are all of these guys his brothers?"

"Most of them, yeah."

"There sure are a lot of them."

"Seven."

Aggie nodded. She'd always wondered what it was like to have a big family. She only had her brother, and they rarely got to see each other.

"Here. It's all set." Nix handed her a piece of paper with the word *Sanctuary* on it and an address.

"What's this?"

"A place where you can get the information you need. It's less than an hour up the road. They know you're coming."

"Thanks, Nix. I knew I could count on you."

"Us girls have to stick together, right?"

"Right."

"Not that it matters, but if Taser asks, were you here?"

"He knows."

"Sean will be disappointed," Nix said with a grin. "He loves pissing Taser off."

Aggie smiled too. "Speaking of, do you have any idea what happened in Honduras?"

"No, Sean won't say, but whatever it was, it must be one hell of a story."

CHAPTER TWENTY-SIX

~ Zeke ~

ZEKE WASN'T CRAZY ABOUT BEING left behind. Nor did he like being out of the loop. He didn't know why Aggie had brought them to some small-town garage, who *Nix* or *Taser* were, or what any of that had to do with their current mission.

Aggie had said to trust her though, and he would, no matter how hard it was, until she gave him a reason not to.

"Sean Callaghan," the muscled mechanic said, holding out his hand.

Zeke took it. "Zeke Ericsson."

"You want to grab a beer, Zeke?"

Zeke's gaze moved to the side, where Aggie had disappeared with the other woman. They were on a schedule. A flexible one, but a schedule, nonetheless. And maybe, just maybe, a tiny part of him worried that Aggie might disappear again if he left despite what she'd said.

"I'll pass."

"It wasn't really a request."

Zeke returned his full attention to the man, even more alert than he had been. The guy was jacked and fit, as if he lifted four-hundred-pound engine blocks and ran ten miles every morning. There was an intensity in his blue gaze and an easy readiness to his body language that smacked of special ops.

The whole situation was getting weirder and weirder.

"Excuse me?"

"Let me enlighten you, Zeke. When my wife said I should take you down to the pub, what she was really saying was, *Vet this guy*. I don't know who your woman is, but Nix obviously does, and she's very protective of those she cares about."

Zeke crossed his arms over his chest and remained where he was, bristling.

"Do you always do what your woman tells you to?"

"Do *you*?" Sean countered. "Seems like you'd rather be in there with her than out here with me, but here we are."

Fuck. The guy had a point.

"Besides," Sean continued, "by the look on your face, you have some questions of your own."

He was right about that too.

"Are you saying you have answers?"

"Maybe."

Zeke considered his options. He could stand in

the parking lot arguing with this guy, or grab a beer and get some information. "Fine."

"Smart man. Nick!" Sean called out. "I'm heading to the pub. Watch the garage, yeah?"

Another man appeared out of the shadows of the garage, looking like a masculine version of Sean's wife. Same dark hair. Same freaky pale eyes.

"You got it."

"Let's go."

Sean started walking down the sidewalk. Zeke fell into step beside him. They didn't speak, which was just fine with him.

A couple of blocks later, they entered Jake's Irish Pub. It was a nice place. Clean and classy yet welcoming, it reminded him of a place he'd visited outside of Dublin once.

Two men, who bore an obvious resemblance to Sean, looked up at their approach from behind the bar. They were older than Zeke by about a decade, give or take, and had the same intense blue eyes and special ops vibe. The younger of the two held a phone to his ear.

Zeke and Sean took seats at the bar. The bigger of the two poured two drafts, placed one in front of Sean and one in front of Zeke, and then looked to Sean expectantly.

"Zeke, these are my brothers, Jake and Ian. Guys, this is Zeke Ericsson."

Sean's tone shifted subtly when he said Zeke's name. Zeke could have sworn their eyes flashed in recognition, which he neither understood nor liked.

Zeke nodded in acknowledgment and said nothing. He didn't know these guys from Adam, and he certainly wasn't accustomed to sharing information.

"Zeke's woman came to see Nix," Sean said conversationally. "She's with her now."

The younger guy—Ian—slipped his phone into his pocket. "Wouldn't by any chance have anything to do with a satellite zoom on Parryville, now would it?"

Zeke's eyes narrowed, and Ian laughed.

"Relax, Zeke," Jake told him. "You're among friends here."

"Is that so?"

"It is, *Raguel*."

"How did you—"

"Not important," Sean said. "What is important is why you need eyes on Parryville."

* * *

Zeke and Sean returned to the garage. His head was swimming. Though he still didn't know a lot about the men he'd just spent the last hour with, he did know that they were a hell of a lot more than they appeared.

Before long, Aggie emerged with the other woman. Both were smiling. Zeke's chest loosened considerably.

"Robin, it's been great seeing you again," Nix said. "Good luck!"

"Thanks."

The two women hugged.

"Think about what I said, okay? Trust your instincts."

It might have been his imagination, but he could have sworn he saw a blush creep up Aggie's cheeks when she answered, "I will."

The dark-haired woman went to her husband's side.

Aggie came to his. "Ready?"

"Yeah, I'm ready."

He opened the passenger door and she climbed in, then he made his way around to the driver's side. He wanted to ask questions, but he wasn't sure where to start.

"We've got to make one more stop before we head to Parryville," she said as they pulled out of the garage lot and onto the road.

"To Sanctuary, I know. Sean filled me in. Sort of. You've got some interesting friends."

Aggie grinned broadly. "That I do."

The ride to Sanctuary was a nice one with mountain roads and unspoiled scenic vistas. They drove with the windows down, filling the interior with clean air and the scents of sunshine and pine.

Zeke wasn't sure what he had expected, but it sure as hell wasn't a sprawling resort that looked more like an exclusive country club getaway. The

Callaghans had said it was a facility for former servicemen and women, run by vets, for vets. It didn't look like any military facility Zeke had ever seen.

A man was waiting for them when they arrived. He introduced himself as Matt Winston and invited them inside. "Zeke and Robin, I presume?"

Zeke couldn't help but notice that these people only seemed to know Aggie by her code name, which was telling.

"Right in one," Aggie said with a smile. "I hope we're not intruding."

"Not at all. Ian told us you'd be coming. The satellite's not quite in place yet. Cage will let us know when it is. It shouldn't be long."

"What smells so good?" Aggie asked.

"Kate's chicken pot pie," Matt said with a knowing grin. "Best there is. How about we wait in the dining room and you can see for yourself?"

Zeke opened his mouth to decline, but Aggie spoke first. "That would be wonderful, thank you. We haven't eaten yet, and it'll save us a stop later."

The dining room was open and airy, with lots of windows and lots of plants.

"Help yourself," Matt said, sweeping his hand toward a buffet table.

Unsurprisingly, Aggie loaded her plate with fresh fruits and vegetables. "These are so good," she moaned around a mouthful of cucumbers and tomatoes.

"We grow mostly everything in our on-site greenhouses or in our orchard," Matt told them. "We're pretty self-sustaining here."

"So, this is a place for vets, huh?" she asked.

Matt nodded and looked meaningfully at Zeke. "It's hard, making the adjustment from active service to civilian. Hard to find your place sometimes. We try to make that process a little easier."

That was something Zeke understood all too well. His own adjustment had been jarring and disorienting, and it had taken a while to find his footing. He still wasn't sure he completely had. "How so?"

"We give them a safe place to stay, let them figure out what's next, then do everything we can to help them achieve that. It's a work in progress. My wife recently started a program to integrate Sanctuary with the community. It's been well received on both sides."

Matt's phone vibrated, and he glanced at the screen. "Cage said everything's ready."

"Perfect timing," Aggie said. "I couldn't possibly eat another bite."

Matt grinned at this, then led them to a conference room. Well, Matt called it a conference room, but it looked more like a high-tech command center to Zeke. One large screen was mounted in the center of the wall with half a dozen smaller screens around it. Each screen had a different picture, and

Zeke recognized them for what they were. Surveillance footage of the buildings and property.

He couldn't help but wonder why they needed that kind of surveillance.

"Zeke, Robin, this is Cage, our resident IT guru."

An auburn-haired guy with bright green eyes turned away from a bank of monitors, laptops, and tablets and smiled. "Nice to meet you. Ian said you wanted a real-time high-def look at some mountains outside of Parryville. Are you looking for something in particular?"

"Some*one*," Aggie clarified.

The guy nodded as if it wasn't an unusual request. "No problem."

Cage tapped a few keys, and an aerial image appeared on the screen. Then, he zeroed in to cover just the mountains they were interested in, which amounted to several hundred square miles. The tree canopy was thick, making it difficult to see the ground in many areas. As far as hiding places went, it was a good one.

Cage superimposed a grid over the image and panned section by section in a methodical sweep. Zeke concentrated on those areas that seemed the most likely places to hole up, knowing exactly what to look for. He'd performed the same tasks for his SEAL team hundreds of times, having analyzed mountains, jungles, deserts, and war-torn cities. In none of those cases had the intel been so clear or current.

"Can you zoom in on A24, C8, and F13?" he asked.

"Sure. I'll layer in some thermal imaging scans, too, though I'm not sure how helpful they'll be. There's probably a decent amount of big game in those woods." Cage tapped more buttons.

"There," Zeke said, pointing to an area with a natural rock formation. "If he's hiding anywhere, it's there."

CHAPTER TWENTY-SEVEN

~ *Aggie* ~

AGGIE REMOVED THE TOWEL FROM her head, then finger-combed out the tangles. Zeke was at the desk, studying the images Cage had printed out for him. He'd been quiet, even more so than usual, since leaving Sanctuary.

She moved across the room and rested her hands on his shoulders. "What are you thinking?"

He sighed at her touch. "That Higgins has dug himself in pretty good. He couldn't have picked a better spot. It makes me wonder if he just got lucky or if there's more to this guy than we know. Either way, it'd be smart not to underestimate him."

"Agreed. I did that once, and it didn't turn out too well."

Zeke wrapped his hand around her wrist and tugged her down onto his lap. She went willingly, relishing the feel of his warm, hard body. It was reassuring.

"Are we going to talk about today?" he asked.

She offered him a small smile. "A lot happened

today. You'll have to be more specific than that."

"All right. Let's start with the fact that your friends have access to state-of-the-art, military-grade technology."

She'd wondered how long it would take him to ask. "I can't tell you everything you want to know, I'm sorry. Those aren't my secrets to share. What I can tell you is, they're good people, and they're not on anyone's books."

He considered that for a moment, then nodded. "How do you know them, and why are they so willing to help you, no questions asked?"

"You ask really good questions," she murmured, pressing a kiss to his lips. She was tempted to do more, but they had to have this conversation. "Believe it or not, there's a network of people who see the issues we face every day and know that the systems put into place to deal with them are broken. They take it upon themselves to do what they can, knowing they have to do it outside of *proper* channels. Much like you do but on a greater scale."

"What do you mean, like me? I'm a mercenary, remember?"

She laughed softly. "Right, *Raguel*."

He tensed and narrowed his eyes. "What do you know about Raguel?"

"I know he was a highly decorated, highly respected, skilled tracker. I know his team was compromised on a mission in the Middle East, and that good men died." He flinched, and she softened her voice. "I know he signed a confession that said he betrayed his team and his country when he didn't. What I don't know is, *why*."

Zeke grasped her around the waist and lifted her off his lap. Then, he stood and began to pace around the room, prowling like an angsty panther. "Given what I know about your friends, I guess I don't need to ask how you know about that."

"Tell me," she said quietly.

"I can't talk about that."

"You *can*," she insisted. "Who are you protecting?"

"Who says I'm protecting anyone?"

"It's the only thing that makes sense. You're a good man, Zeke, and I don't believe you'd betray anyone for your own personal gain. But I have no trouble believing you'd sacrifice yourself for someone you cared about."

When he continued to remain quiet, she said, "I can find out, you know."

Concern flashed in his eyes. "You need to stay out of it."

"I think we both know that's not going to happen. You might as well just tell me. Who are you protecting?"

"Myself," he said with a scowl. "My … family."

She sat up straight. No one had said anything about Zeke having a family. "Please don't tell me you're married."

"I'm not married."

"Kids?"

"No."

"Parents, then? Siblings?"

He ground his teeth but said nothing. He didn't have to. His eyes spoke for him. They were filled with pain. Pain and regret.

"When's the last time you saw them?"

"Does it fucking matter?" he snapped. "Let me answer that for you. No, it doesn't."

"Why did you say you did something if you didn't?" she pressed.

"You said it yourself. The system is broken. I didn't betray my team, but someone had to take the blame."

"Why you?"

"Because I had the most incentive to do so."

"I don't understand," she said, exasperated and frustrated and wanting to help.

"You're not going to let this go, are you?" He exhaled heavily. "Okay, look. I'm going to say this once, then I never want to talk about it again, got it?"

She nodded, even though she wasn't sure she could keep that promise.

"My father was an abusive piece of shit, a runner for the local mob. He skimmed off the top and got two bullets in the back of the head for his trouble, leaving my mother with three kids and no income. We moved to a trailer park, where my mother did what she had to do to put food on the table and clothes on our backs. She cleaned for people and did laundry, but it wasn't enough. She learned she could make more money doing other things."

Aggie could guess what those things were based on his dark scowl.

"I was the oldest. My job was to keep my sisters out of the way while my mother ... *worked*. When I got old enough, I started picking up odd jobs. It helped, but as you might imagine, honest work was hard to find for a kid, and I'd made a promise to my mother not to get involved with the local wise guys. I enlisted the day I turned eighteen and made arrangements to have my pay sent to my mother and sisters. I told my mother she didn't have to work anymore, that I'd take care of them financially, and I did. They weren't rich or anything, but it was something, Things were looking up. Eventually, they were able to even put a down payment on a small house in a nice neighborhood. My sisters got part-time jobs and student loans and were going to college."

He paused.

"I'd been out of the country for months when the mission I was on went to hell. When I woke up weeks later, I found out that my mother had been diagnosed with cancer, and that both of my sisters had left school to get full time jobs in order to care for her and pay for treatment, but they were still racking up debt like crazy and about to lose the house."

Zeke moved to the window and stared out. "My CO came to me in the hospital and told me that they had evidence I had compromised the team—taped conversations, incriminating videos, money exchanges. It was all bullshit, but you know how it is. In the service, truth is what your CO says it is. He told me if I signed a confession, he'd make sure my family was taken care of, and I'd get to walk away quietly with a dishonorable discharge. It was a no-brainer. I was looking at months of rehab and a military trial that I had little hope of winning."

Aggie's heart broke for him. It was as she'd suspected. He'd sacrificed everything.

"Do they know?" she asked. "Your family?"

"No. They think I died over there, and the money they received was part of my death benefits. If they knew the truth, it would crush them."

Aggie moved behind him, wrapping her arms around him and pressing against his back. She made a silent promise to do whatever she could to bring the real betrayer to justice.

"Thank you for sharing that with me. You're a good man, Zeke Ericsson."

He grunted.

"Have I ever told you how sexy that is?" she said softly, letting her hands trail down his chest and over his abs, then slipping them into his pants.

She was thrilled to feel him twitch and begin to harden in her hands.

She would discover the truth and make things right, but at that moment, all she wanted was to make him forget everything, except the pleasure she could give him.

* * *

"I'm going after Higgins alone," Zeke informed her the next day. "I'll bring him to the rendezvous point. Stay safe and out of sight."

Aggie didn't argue. While she might enjoy new adventures, she would only slow him down. He leaned in for a quick peck, but she cupped the back of his head and gave him a proper kiss.

"What was that for?" he asked.

"Incentive. A reminder of what's waiting for you."

He grinned and slipped out of the vehicle. Within seconds, he disappeared into the woods.

Aggie drove away and did what she did best. She found a quiet place and linked up her computer. She had no idea how long it would take Zeke to find Sam and bring him back out. Even with the footage and the plan, Zeke had warned her it could take a while. The area where they believed Sam was hiding was miles away from any access road.

That was one of the reasons she'd insisted he wear the cuff with the tracking device in it. She'd be watching over him the whole time.

She had complete confidence in Zeke. If Sam was in there, Zeke would find him. According to T, he was among the best of the best, and T did not make claims like that lightly.

Best-case scenario: Sam was alive and in hiding. Aggie had no doubt that she could convince Sam to share his inside information, and if he did that, she'd be able to take it from there. The trickiest part would be getting Sam somewhere safe, perhaps with a new identity. Luckily, she had plenty of people who could help with that.

Worst-case scenario: someone else had gotten to Sam first. She didn't want to think about that.

CHAPTER TWENTY-EIGHT

~ Zeke ~

Once in the woods, Zeke let his training take over. He moved swiftly and quietly, managing to cover a lot of ground in a short amount of time. The falling rain was an advantage; he didn't have to worry as much about being seen or heard.

He welcomed the focus and the calming effect it had on him.

Have an objective. Achieve it. Move on.

That worked for him. That was how he lived his life. Clean. Simple.

The last few months had been anything but clean or simple. He no longer had a clear objective. He didn't know what, if any, part he played, going forward.

And it was all because of *her*.

Being around Aggie had muddied the waters significantly. His feelings for her were complicated enough, but thinking about the last forty-eight hours made his head spin. He'd thought he had a grasp on things, but it'd turned out, he didn't have a fucking clue.

As he neared the target site, he was pleased with what he discovered. A sequence of freshly dug holes, probably for waste. A decided lack of kindling on the ground around the area. And the faint but unmistakable aromas of wood smoke and roasted rabbit.

This, he could do. This was second nature.

He approached the overhang carefully and without sound and found exactly what he'd come for.

"Sam Higgins."

The man tending the fire looked up, his eyes wild. He was thinner than the images Zeke had seen, and he was sporting a full beard, but it was the same guy.

Higgins reached for his rifle.

"I wouldn't do that if I were you," Zeke warned.

Higgins looked at the Sig in Zeke's hand and stilled.

"Who are you? What do you want?"

"I'm a friend of Aggie's. What I want is information."

Higgins narrowed his eyes. "What kind of information?"

Zeke stepped farther in and picked up the rifle, placing it out of Higgins's reach, then tucked his gun into the back of his pants. Higgins was no threat. The guy looked like a good stiff breeze would knock him over.

"Let's start with whatever sent a bunch of thugs to grab Aggie out of her bed and beat the shit out of her."

Higgins dropped his gaze. "Is she okay?"

Regret tinged Higgins's voice, but what Zeke didn't hear was surprise or outrage. He closed the distance between them and punched Higgins right in the mouth. Higgins stumbled back, hit the wall of rock, and went down on his ass.

"You knew they would go after her, didn't you, you fucking weasel?"

"No! I mean ... yeah, I thought they might toss her apartment or something, but I didn't think they'd hurt her. She wasn't part of it."

Zeke reached down, hauled him up by his filthy shirt, and hit him again, sending him back to the ground. "But they didn't know that, did they? What are they looking for?"

Higgins leaned to the side and spit out a mouthful of blood. "They'll kill me if I tell you."

"*I'll* kill you if you don't."

"It's complicated!" Higgins whined.

"Then, let me simplify things. I know you and your guys were running shipments of toxic waste to illegal dump sites run by the mob. I know the FBI approached you about being an informant. What I don't know is why you ghosted and left Aggie in their crosshairs."

Higgins's eyes widened. "Who *are* you?"

"Your worst fucking nightmare if you don't convince me that you're worth more alive than you are dead. Start. Talking."

Zeke took another step forward, and Higgins put up both hands.

"All right, all right! You're right, okay? About everything. I was making runs. They didn't really give me much of a choice. It was do what they said and get cash in my pocket or lose my job—or worse. I didn't feel right about it, but what was I supposed to do? If I didn't, they'd just find someone else."

"Tell me about the FBI."

Higgins shrugged. "A guy just showed up at my door one day. Said he was a fed, investigating the plant, and that if I helped them, they'd help me. I figured it was a way out."

"But it wasn't."

Higgins shook his head. "It was at first. The agent assigned to my case—Paul Hanlon—seemed like a stand-up guy. I was supposed to keep track of everything, and I did. Notes, names, pictures, all of it, on this flash drive they gave me. I was going to hand it over, but Hanlon didn't show. Another agent did. He asked me for the drive, but something felt off, you know? So, I told him I wasn't stupid enough to keep it with me, that I had it hidden and couldn't get it until later. They must have seen me with Aggie and figured I'd given the drive to her for safe keeping. Anyway, he said he needed to show me something. Turned out, what he wanted to show me was a picture of the first guy's body being fished out of the river."

"So, you ran."

"Fuck yes, I ran! Wouldn't you?"

"Where's the information now? Do you still have it?"

"No." He spit again.

"You're lying."

Higgins rallied and looked up at Zeke with defiance. "What if I am? Are you going to shoot me?"

"Tempting, but no. Aggie wants me to bring you back alive."

"Aggie? Why?"

"Because for some unknown reason, she wants to help you."

"I told you, no one can help me. My only chance is to disappear."

"I found you. Eventually, they will too. Are you going to live like a hermit for the rest of your life, always looking over your shoulder, waking up every morning and wondering if it's going to be the day they find you?"

"It's not so bad," Higgins said, though his voice lacked conviction. "I've got plenty of food and water. I don't have to deal with anyone's shit or follow anyone else's rules. I'll keep moving. The Appalachians run a long way."

"Yeah, well, I'm not asking. Get up. You're coming with me."

"I don't think so."

Zeke sighed. If the guy insisted on doing things the hard way, he'd oblige.

Zeke was just about to haul him to his feet when the leather wrist cuff Aggie had given him began to vibrate. She had insisted he wear it, so she could keep track of his progress and warn him of impending danger.

He had resisted at first. If things did go south, he didn't want Aggie venturing into the woods, looking for him. But then she'd looked at him with those pretty hazel eyes while sinking down onto his shaft, and he hadn't been able to say no. Hell, he would have agreed to practically anything at that point.

He held up his hand, warning Higgins to be quiet, and listened, but it was impossible to hear anything over the rain.

He signaled to Higgins to stay put, then moved toward the opening. Keeping his body in shadow, he pulled a scope out and scanned the area. The rain had intensified, coming down in big, fat drops.

Zeke spotted movement about a hundred yards beyond—two dark smudges against the green and the gray. He sensed Higgins creeping up behind him and glanced back in warning.

Higgins held up both hands to show they were empty and whispered, "What's happening?"

"We've got company," he answered equally quietly and handed Higgins the scope. "Friends of yours?"

"That's the agent who wasted Hanlon and threatened to do the same to me. His name's Manelli. I don't know the other guy."

"Hey, over there!" the unknown guy said, his voice muffled by the rain.

"Check it out," Manelli said.

The unknown guy moved closer. "Looks like a cave or something."

"Fuck. What do we do?" Higgins asked.

Zeke considered their options and realized they didn't have many. "Stay here," he commanded, pulling the camo hood up over his head.

"Are you nuts? Where are you going? They'll kill me!"

"No, they won't."

Zeke slipped out from the overhang and stayed close to the rocks. He crouched behind the scrub that flanked the opening. The two men approached, Manelli bringing up the rear.

"Samuel Higgins. This is Agent William Banks of the FBI. Come out slowly, hands where I can see them."

Zeke had no idea if Banks was dirty, but he knew Manelli was, which meant if Higgins surrendered, he was as good as dead. He wasn't about to let that happen.

Apparently Higgins had the same thought.

"Why?" Higgins shouted from within. "So you can waste me like you did Hanlon? I don't think so."

"Nice try, Higgins. We know you pulled the trigger. The guy had a wife and kids, did you know that?"

A shot rang out, and Banks dropped like a stone. Manelli stepped closer, pointed his gun at Banks's prone form, and fired again.

"Enough of that." Manelli approached the opening. "Hello, Sam. You know why I'm here. Give me the drive."

"And what, you'll just let me walk away?"

A dark laugh. "I think we both know that's not going to happen. You killed two federal agents, and in the course of evading capture, you were mortally wounded. The only question is, whether or not your death was the result of an instant kill shot to the head or a shot to the stomach, causing you to bleed out slowly and painfully over the course of the next several hours."

"How about C, none of the above?" Zeke offered.

Before Manelli could turn around, Zeke disabled him with a swift and brutal strike to the head. He kicked Manelli's gun to the side, and then he pulled zip ties from one of his deep pockets and tossed a few to Higgins.

"Get his feet, then help me drag him farther into the cave."

Higgins's hands were shaking, and he looked like he was going to be sick, but he did what Zeke told him to do.

Zeke studied Manelli's face, remembering Aggie's description of the man who'd hit her. Pale, pockmarked skin, check. Dark, close-cropped hair and darker eyes, check. A wide nose that looked as if it had been broken a few times, check. A faint, thin scar that ran from his left ear to his jaw. Check and check.

Cold fury welled inside him. He broke Manelli's nose, dislocated his ankles, broke the fingers of his dominant hand, and, remembering Aggie's bruises, turned him on his side and delivered several swift kicks to the guy's kidneys. Sam stared at him with wide, scared eyes.

"This is the guy who hurt Aggie," Zeke explained.

"Oh," Sam said, his expression turning angry. "In that case…" Sam pulled his leg back and delivered a few kicks of his own. "What about the other guy?"

Zeke shook his head. "We can't help him, and we're better off not disturbing the crime scene. Ballistics will show it was Manelli's gun that killed him. Grab your stuff."

"We're just going to leave them here?"

"They didn't come alone, and backup won't be far behind. We don't want to be here when they show up."

This time, Higgins didn't argue.

CHAPTER TWENTY-NINE

~ *Aggie* ~

AGGIE BREATHED A SIGH OF RELIEF when she saw the tracking dot moving again. Nix had sent her an emergency text, warning of FBI activity in the area.

She gathered her things and drove to the agreed-upon meeting point. As quickly as Zeke had disappeared into the woods, he reappeared, only this time, he had Sam Higgins with him.

Zeke ushered Sam into the vehicle, then got in himself. Unable to stop herself, Aggie grabbed his face with both hands and kissed him soundly.

"What was that for?" he asked.

"I was worried."

He seemed to find that amusing.

Aggie glanced in the rearview mirror and caught sight of Sam. He looked awful. She had a feeling that it wasn't just because he'd been living in the wilderness. His eyes were haunted, as if he'd seen things he wished he hadn't.

"Any complications?" she asked Zeke.

"A few. Nothing I couldn't handle."

She nodded, stepped on the accelerator, and drove away. She was sure he'd fill her in later, preferably once Sam spent some quality time with a bar of soap. They followed the route they'd outlined earlier and arrived at the safe house without issue.

"Tell me," she said once Sam was in the shower.

Zeke filled her in.

"Do we need to send someone out there for Manelli?"

"No. I left him a flare gun. He'll signal for help when he comes to. Assuming he doesn't swallow it, that is."

"What now?"

"Here." Zeke placed a thumb drive in her hand. "Let's see what all the fuss is about, then we'll go from there."

Aggie plugged the drive into her laptop. It had everything Sam had said it had—names, dates, schedules, pictures, even a few recorded conversations.

"This is gold," Aggie said, blowing out a breath. "I have a feeling that once I plug in some of these names and follow the money trail, this is going to take us way beyond Parryville."

Sam emerged from the shower, looking—and smelling—better than he had when he went in.

"Aggie, I'm sorry. Zeke told me what happened. I never wanted you to get hurt."

"I know. You're forgiven."

Zeke snorted.

"That's it?" Sam asked, doubt and suspicion clear in his features.

She shrugged. "That's it. You were in a tough situation, and like you said, you didn't mean for it to happen."

Sam started moving toward her, but Zeke glared at him and shook his head. Sam turned around and headed for the tray of sandwiches and coffee instead.

"Feeling a little protective there?" she murmured softly.

He grunted, sending ribbons of warmth into her chest.

* * *

"It's all set," Aggie told Zeke several days later. "Sam's agreed to testify. He's officially in WITSEC, and Manelli will be remanded to a federal holding facility as soon as he recovers from his injuries. Seems like someone really did a number on the guy."

Aggie looked at him expectantly, but Zeke just shrugged. "How'd they get Sam in WITSEC so fast?"

"Remember Matt Winston, the guy at Sanctuary? Well, his wife, Hayley, is a former Deputy US Marshal. She pulled some strings and was able to fast-track everything."

"Your network is vast, Robin Hood. No wonder you're able to remain so elusive."

"*You* found me."

He tilted his head and regarded her. "Did I though?"

"What's that supposed to mean?"

"It means, I'm not an idiot. You weren't some random job. Charley practically handed you to me on a silver platter *and* paid me fifty grand for the privilege. Who is she, Aggie, and why did she do that?"

Aggie couldn't tell him about Charley without telling him about her brother, and she couldn't do that, no matter how much she wanted to. "I can't answer that."

"How about you try? And while you're at it, you can explain how you were able to warn me that the FBI was closing in on us out there with such impeccable timing?"

She opened her mouth, then closed it again. They weren't her secrets to share. "I can't. I'm sorry."

"Can't? Or won't?"

"Can't."

"Then, I'm sorry too."

"What does that mean?"

"It means I'm done with the *need to know* bullshit. You know everything about me and I know nothing about you. I'm done being a pawn in a game I don't understand."

He stared deep into her eyes. "It means, you either trust me or you don't."

His eyes hardened when seconds ticked by and she said nothing. Then he turned around and walked out.

* * *

Aggie stared out at the scenic view, seeing none of it. The chalet had always been her safe place. Her place to go to rest and recharge in between projects.

Not this time. Now, everything reminded her of Zeke. She saw him everywhere. Cooking in the kitchen. Working out in the gym. Naked in her bed.

Weeks had gone by without a word. Every day, her hope faded a little more that she would.

She got it—she really did. She had *a lot* of secrets. Her life and the work she did required anonymity and solitude, neither of which was conducive to a relationship. Her brother was the exception, and that was a secret she'd take to the grave. Not even Nix knew she and T were related. Nix thought Robin Hood was one of T's Chameleons, nothing more.

Until Zeke, that hadn't been a problem. She moved around a lot, changing identities like most women changed their nail color. She met new people, experienced new things, and eventually returned to her home base, feeling like she'd accomplished something.

It had been enough.

Her laptop pinged, signaling a secure message request.

"Speak of the devil, and he doth appear," she quipped as T's face filled the screen.

"You were talking about me?" he asked, amused.

"More like thinking out loud."

"No word from Raguel?"

"No, and I don't think there will be. Are you calling for a reason?"

"Do I need one?"

"Yes."

He sighed. "Fine. I need you to run some financial forensics on a guy named Shelton MacNamarra."

Aggie nodded, grateful for a distraction. It was time she got out of her own head and got back to work. She'd been dragging her feet in picking her next target, knowing that once she did, she'd be gone for months.

"Okay. Am I looking for anything specific?"

"Deposits made from foreign countries, particularly the Middle East and eastern Africa."

"Sure. I'll get right on it."

"Thanks."

"No problem."

CHAPTER THIRTY

~ *Zeke* ~

THE BELL TINKLED OVER THE DOOR at the front of the shop.

Zeke looked up at the old-fashioned analog clock hanging on the wall and cursed. It was well past closing time, which meant Betsy or Becky or whatever the fuck her name was must have forgotten to lock the door. Again.

She was cute, but she wasn't the brightest bulb in the box. She also wasn't going to last the week.

With a sigh, he put down his pencil and turned away from the backpiece he had been designing. It was a custom image, one that would never make it onto anyone's skin because it had been created for one woman, a woman he would never see again.

It had been weeks since he'd walked away. Not an hour went by without him thinking of her. The most he managed was a few minutes here and there.

He kept telling himself that it was for the best. That there was no future with a woman who had more secrets than he did, a woman who didn't trust him enough to share anything with him.

She shared her body with you, a little voice said.

It hadn't been enough. He wanted more.

Zeke stepped out of the back and looked around, ready to tell whoever it was that they were closed and to come back another time. But there was no one there.

He shrugged, locked the door, and headed to the tiny room in the back, the one where he'd been crashing the past week.

The tingle of warning came too late. A sharp jab in the side of his neck was followed immediately by a black hood being pulled over his head. His struggles were in vain. He got his hand briefly around one thick neck but was out before he hit the ground.

* * *

When Zeke came to, it was to find himself strapped in a helicopter. The black hood was still over his head, but he could hear the muffled sound of the rotors through the earphones that had been placed around his ears and feel the synchronous pulsing vibrations through the seat.

He tested his hands—bound. His feet—also bound.

He didn't know who had him or why, only that he was going to cause them a world of hurt when he found out.

They remained airborne for about an hour, according to his internal clock. As he regained more of his faculties, he had vague, hazy recollections of being moved from a vehicle, onto a plane, and now, a chopper. Whoever it was, they were going to a lot of effort to get him somewhere.

Within moments of landing, his earphones were removed, as was his hood, and Zeke found himself glaring into the blurry face of Sean Callaghan.

"Oh, he doesn't look happy," said another voice cheerily.

Zeke blinked, certain he was seeing double because there were now *two* Sean Callaghans peering at him.

"What the actual fuck is going on?" he managed. His mouth was dry, his tongue thick.

"You wanted answers. You're going to get them." Sean One slid a Bowie knife smoothly from the sheath. He sliced through the bindings with two quick swipes, freeing Zeke's hands and feet.

Zeke fumbled with the harness—his fingers weren't cooperating fully—and attempted to lunge out of the chopper. He fell promptly on his face. Apparently, his legs weren't fully cooperating yet either.

"Jesus. How much did you give him?" said Sean Two, sidestepping out of Zeke's reach in an easy glide.

"Enough to get him here. Grab his arm and

help me get him inside."

They half-dragged, half-carried Zeke toward a cabin. The sun was just coming over the horizon, and Zeke tried to get his bearings, but there was nothing remotely recognizable. They appeared to be in the middle of nowhere.

Zeke was taken inside and strong-armed into a seated position on a sofa.

"Here, drink this. It'll help."

"Nix," he said, recognizing the face of the woman holding out a tumbler.

She smirked. "Aw, you remember. Seriously, drink this. Mick's hangover cure will do wonders for that headache you must be feeling, and you're going to want a clear head for this."

Zeke's hands flexed. Sean One and Sean Two watched him carefully. Sean One shook his head ever so slightly in warning. In his current state, he couldn't fight off a little old lady with a walker, let alone the Seans and Nix, who was probably the most dangerous of the three.

"For what?" Zeke ground out.

"Why did you walk away from Robin?"

"None of your fucking business."

"I thought so. You're spooked, right? She trusted you enough to give you a glimpse into her life, and it scared the shit out of you." Nix tilted her head thoughtfully. "I expected more from you, Raguel."

"She doesn't trust me. She didn't tell me

anything."

Nix's eyes flashed. "No, she didn't, because she'd rather die than betray us. But she *does* trust you. Otherwise, she never would have brought you with her to meet us. She would have ditched your ass, gotten the information, then met up with you again outside of Parryville. She could have done it, you know. Easily."

He blinked. Nix took a swig from the tumbler, presumably to demonstrate that it wasn't drugged, and then held it out to him again. This time, he took it. Within minutes, his headache disappeared, and clarity returned.

"It was a test?" he guessed.

"She had to know if you could handle it."

"Handle *what* exactly?"

"Her life. No doubt you've put enough pieces together to figure out she's no ordinary woman."

Yeah, he'd figured that out pretty quick.

"Listen, what we do, it's important. It requires trust and faith and absolute secrecy. I don't think you understand the risk Robin took in bringing you with her. She wouldn't have taken the risk if she didn't believe in you."

Sean Two handed him an envelope.

"What's this?"

"Open it."

He did. Inside were satellite photos. Financial records that showed huge transfers of money into offshore bank accounts. Shipment records of highly classified weapons that had been re-routed. Satellite surveillance images of a man meeting with rebel leaders, a man Zeke knew all too well.

It was proof. Proof that he hadn't done what they'd said he did. Proof that his team's commanding officer, Shelton MacNamarra, had.

"How did you get this?"

Sean's lips curled. "It's what we do. Except for the financial stuff. That was all Robin. She followed the money trail and gave us the names we needed to get everything else."

"Robin did," Zeke echoed, his throat drying up again.

"Yeah, man. Try to keep up, will you? Who do you think asked us to look into this? MacNamarra's just the tip of a very dirty iceberg. It's a work in progress, but you've been cleared of all wrongdoing."

His head was swimming, and it wasn't because of whatever they'd shot into his neck. If what they were saying was true ...

"Oh, and you might be interested in this, too." Nix handed him another envelope, then watched intently as he removed the contents. Confirmation that the mortgage on his mother's house had been paid off. A notice that his mother had been accepted into a new treatment program and was responding well. Pictures of his sisters on a college campus.

"I need to talk to her."

"Yes, you do," agreed Nix, "but that might be a

problem."

"Why?"

"Because no one knows where she is. She disappeared right after she asked us to look into that," Nix said, waving toward the file.

"I'll find her."

"No, you won't," Nix said with a laugh. "But she'll resurface again eventually, and if you're even half as smart as I think you are, you'll be waiting for her when she does."

CHAPTER THIRTY-ONE

~ *Aggie* ~

AGGIE FELT NONE OF THE USUAL anticipation as she worked her way back to the chalet, just a vague sense of dread. Too many memories lingered there, memories that included more than just the peace and solitude the place provided. Zeke hadn't spent a lot of time there, but he'd certainly left an impression.

Over the past few months, she'd gotten used to the idea that Zeke was no longer part of her life. The ache remained, however, a constant presence deep in her chest. She carried it with her—a painful reminder that her life had never been and would never be normal.

Perhaps that was why she'd stayed away as long as she had. She'd known that returning to the chalet would bring those feelings to the surface. But after spending three months in a crowded city, bombarded by people and noise, overcome by the sheer sensory overload, she needed a break to recharge, and the chalet was the one place to do that safely and without fear of discovery.

Well, she hoped that was still the case. Zeke knew about the place, which, strictly speaking, meant the location was now compromised.

Zeke would not betray me that way.

Nor did she believe he would betray her friends. Not that he knew anything specific, but he knew enough to cast unwanted attention their way if he wanted to.

Aggie had warned Nix when she sent the information on McNamarra's bank accounts, just in case. That was a fun conversation. Nix had told her not to worry about it, but how could she not? She had so few friends. So few people who knew anything about her. And none of them, not even her brother, knew *everything*.

Her existence was a solitary one, and most of the time, she liked it that way.

T liked to say she was a human conduit, a funnel through which great quantities of information and emotions flowed. Sometimes, bits and pieces got trapped, and over time, she reached capacity and needed to *clean her filter* to function properly again.

He also said she was a glutton for punishment, putting herself in the midst of situations where she connected most with those she was trying to help.

He wasn't wrong. She'd always been that way, particularly with negative emotions. She felt those more strongly than the others, which was probably why she was compelled to do what she did. Living among them. Getting to know them. Experiencing firsthand the effects of greed and corruption at the lowest level made it real in a way that sitting behind a screen in a luxurious refuge never could.

Unfortunately, she could only do it for several months at a time before she became overwhelmed.

Meditation helped, as did sticking to a primarily organic diet, but eventually, she needed to distance herself from everyone and everything.

Simply put, being around people drained her.

Well, being around most people did. Zeke was an exception, which was why Nix's words had struck such a chord with her. Aggie felt *different* around Zeke. When she was with him, she felt connected to another human being in a way that didn't drain her, but fortified her.

"Your soul mate. Your perfect match."

Nix's words echoed in her head for the billionth time. It was a nice thought, but soul mates didn't walk out and disappear so easily, did they?

Aggie arrived at the chalet in darkness, too tired to do much of anything besides shower and crawl into bed. She slept a solid twelve hours and probably would have slept even longer if her bladder hadn't been close to rupturing.

With sunlight streaming in through the windows, she yawned and made her way to the coffee machine. Part of her had hoped—irrationally—that Zeke might be waiting for her, but everything was just as she'd left it.

Wherever he was, she hoped he was happy. She hadn't been in contact with Nix, so she had no idea what, if anything, had come from the information she'd sent her way.

Aggie started the machine, then foraged for something to eat. She added a call to the delivery service to her list of things to do.

She found some trail mix and sat at the breakfast counter, trying not to think of how Zeke had perched her on it more than once and snacked on *her*.

That was when she saw it. A business card, propped up against a tiny crystal vase. Linen, with pearly-white raised holographic lettering. *Archangel Ink*.

Her heart began to pound furiously as she reached for it. She turned it over, registering the handwritten message scrawled on the back.

Good for one custom tattoo. Must present in person to redeem.

* * *

Aggie shoved her hands into her pockets and looked at the shop on the other side of the street. It looked like a classy place, far removed from some of the dives she'd seen in her travels.

The street-facing window was large and tinted black with the same holographic image on the card.

She watched as a steady stream of people came and went, dwindling as the hours ticked by. It seemed to do good business, but she wasn't surprised. She'd seen some of Zeke's drawings. He was an extremely talented artist.

Just do it, Aggie.

Drawing a deep breath, she summoned her courage, crossed the street, and walked inside.

It was like entering an art museum. A semicircular reception desk sat just inside. Behind it, a spectacular mural of a fierce angel warrior, wings spread, sword in hand, ready to do some damage. To the left, a waiting area with leather seating and framed artwork. Two small, matching, curved desks were there as well, where clients could look through designs in binders and discuss options with artists.

What Aggie didn't see were actual tattoo stations, but she could hear muted conversations and buzzing from the back.

An extremely attractive young woman came out of the back and smiled in welcome. "Welcome to Archangel. Can I help you?"

"Hi. Yeah." Aggie pulled the card out of her pocket and handed it to the woman.

The woman's eyes widened, and then her grin grew. "You must be Aggie. He's been hoping you'd come."

CHAPTER THIRTY-TWO

~ *Zeke* ~

"All done." Zeke finished up the sleeve and sat back. "Check it out," he said, waving a gloved hand toward the trifold mirror.

The canvas got up and stood in front of the mirror, turning to view the image from all angles.

Zeke gave his back a stretch and cracked his neck. Both were stiff from being hunched over for so long. He'd been working sixteen-hour days, and he still had a waiting list.

He couldn't keep up the pace much longer. The only reason he'd been putting in as many hours as he had was because he hoped Aggie would show.

Six months. That was how long it had been since he'd walked away. Four, since he'd had that unexpected meet and greet with Nix and the deadly duo.

He wiped down his station and glanced at the clock. Closing time. Another day that Aggie hadn't shown.

Zeke started each day with the hope that she would, but as time went on, he had to face the possibility that it wasn't going to happen.

Surely, she'd been back to the chalet by now. Surely, she'd seen the card.

Unless something had happened.

His chest tightened, just like it always did when that possibility entered his mind. And just like always, he flashed back to the first time he'd seen her in that farmhouse, bruised and battered yet feisty enough to save herself. Yeah, he'd shown up in time to help and maybe expedite things a little, but he had no doubt she would have done just fine without him.

And that was the problem right there, wasn't it? She didn't need him. She could walk away at any moment without a backward glance.

So, he'd done it first.

Except he had been looking back, every fucking day.

Who was watching her back these days?

Nobody, according to Nix. Yeah, he'd called Callaghan Auto. Multiple times. Wanting to know if there'd been any word. Zeke could handle Aggie being pissed. Hell, she *should* be pissed. But if something had happened, something that could have been prevented if he hadn't walked away ...

He'd already made up his mind. He'd give it another day, two at most, and if he still hadn't heard anything, then he would haul his ass to Pine Ridge and demand answers. They could say they didn't know anything, but he didn't believe for one moment that they couldn't find out.

"It's fucking awesome, man," the canvas said, stepping away from the mirror and bringing Zeke out of his own head. "Worth every penny."

Zeke nodded, accepting the praise. It *was* a damn good piece.

He applied a thin layer of salve and wrapped the fresh ink with a sterile bandage, then walked the guy to the front, mindlessly repeating the aftercare instructions, knowing the guy probably wouldn't follow them for more than a day or two, if that.

The guy paid and left. There was nothing left for Zeke to do but head out, grab something to eat at the twenty-four-hour place up the road, then catch a few Zs before he did it all again.

"Flip the sign and turn out the lights, Cass. We're done."

"You've got one more," Cass said to him, tilting her head toward the waiting area.

Zeke shook his head. He was beat, and at two a.m., chances were, whoever it was had come straight from the nearest bar. "Tell them to come back tomorrow."

"Tell her yourself."

Zeke was about to say something else when he felt it. A tingling at the back of his neck—a sure sign that he was in someone's sights. He raised his gaze to Cass, saw her smirk.

He turned slowly and saw a woman sitting there, flipping through one of the binders that held his designs.

Aggie.

Relief flooded through him in a wave powerful enough to almost take him to his knees. Relief and disbelief and an incredible sense of joy.

She smiled at him. "Hey."

"Hey."

He remained rooted to the spot, afraid to move, for fear she'd disappear. She got to her feet, placed the binder back on the table, and shoved her hands in her pockets. She looked as nervous as he felt as she closed the distance between them.

She stopped short of where he stood and held up the business card he'd left at the chalet. "I'm interested in getting a tattoo."

"Are you now?" he murmured.

Aggie was there. Within touching distance. Smiling at him.

She nodded. "I hear you're the best."

As far as she was concerned, he was also the only. No one was going to touch that pristine skin of hers besides him.

"Got something in mind?"

"A few ideas," she said almost shyly, "but I'm open to suggestions."

That was good. Perhaps he'd even show her the full-body pieces he'd designed for her. She could pick and choose some or all. But later.

He couldn't stand it any longer. One moment, there was three feet between them. The next, she was in his arms, and he was kissing her like she was the air he needed to breathe. Her arms curled around his neck and she kissed him back just as desperately.

"I missed you," he murmured against her lips.

"I missed you too."

"Want to get out of here?"

Her eyes flashed with a familiar heat, and she licked her lips, now slightly red and swollen. "What about my tattoo?"

"Later," he growled, grabbing her hand and tugging her out of the shop with Cass looking on in amusement.

They made it as far as the sidewalk before he backed her up against the building and kissed her again.

"I have a hotel room a block away," she said breathlessly.

"Works for me."

* * *

An hour later, Aggie lay beside him, half-draped over his body, petting his chest with soft, gentle strokes.

"Déjà vu," she said. "You, me, a hotel room."

He kissed the top of her head and pulled her tighter against him. "I guess we did spend a lot of time in hotel rooms and moving vehicles, huh?"

"Story of my life," she said on an exhale. "Neither one of us is content to stay in one place for very long."

"No," he agreed.

"Zeke?"

"Yeah?"

"Why did you leave?"

He'd asked himself the same thing time and time again, and he'd kept coming back to the same answer.

"You have this whole other life, Aggie, and I couldn't figure out where I fit into it, if at all."

"Seems pretty obvious to me."

"Enlighten me."

She crawled on top of him, and then she folded her arms under her chin and pierced him with those haunting eyes. She fit so perfectly, her delicate, soft curves molding to his harder planes.

"By my side. On top of me. Beneath me. In my kitchen, making me breakfast."

He smiled and placed his large palms over her rounded backside, then sobered again. "I'm serious, Aggie. You don't need me."

"*Need* is such a subjective word, isn't it?" she mused. "I mean, can I continue to exist without you in my life? Sure. But I don't *want* to."

He knew exactly what she meant because he felt the same way. Without Aggie, he'd continued to function, but it hadn't been a happy existence. He had done what he needed to do, nothing more, nothing less.

"You're beautiful. Smart. Compassionate. Wealthy as fuck and part of a powerful network. What could you possibly want from me?"

Her eyes softened. "Don't you know?"

He had a pretty good idea, but he needed to hear her say it. "Tell me."

"You're my *croie*."

"Your what?"

"That's what Nix calls it. It's an adaptation of the Irish word for heart. A soul mate. The one person with whom you share a unique bond. A perfect complement. The yin to my yang. The—"

"Okay, okay, I get it." He laughed softly.

"At least, I *think* you are."

"You think? You're not sure?"

"There's only one way to be sure."

"Oh yeah? What's that?"

"According to Nix, it works both ways. You can't be my *croie* if I'm not yours. So, am I?"

Zeke rolled her over and looked into her eyes as he slid deep inside her.

"Yes, Aggie. You most definitely are."

EPILOGUE – PART I

~ *Aggie* ~

"So?" Nix asked quietly. They sat wrapped in fluffy robes, sipping champagne and enjoying a spa day at the Celtic Goddess luxury resort on the outskirts of Pine Ridge. Nix knew the owners and had reserved a private room for her and Aggie. The pampering was exactly what she'd needed. When she climbed into bed with Zeke later that night, buffed and waxed with skin smoother than a baby's bottom, she thought he'd appreciate it, too.

"So…" A smile curled Aggie's lips, just as it always did when she thought of Zeke and the way things were between them. "You were right. He's the one."

Nix nodded, pleased but not surprised. "Good."

"It's weird, you know? I never expected this. Any of this."

"Yes, I know. I've got *kids* for God's sake."

Aggie laughed. She didn't know anything about Nix's origins, who she'd been or what circumstances had put her in Taser's sights, just like Nix didn't know about hers. Chameleons didn't talk about their past histories. Once they signed on, they got new lives, new identities.

Nix was one of the best agents her brother had ever had. She still was. There was a time when that meant no commitments, no friends, no family, but Nix proved that it was possible to have it all. The key, according to Nix, was finding the right one. Someone who would support but not suffocate.

There was no doubt in Aggie's mind that Zeke was the right one for her. She couldn't imagine a day without him. He was her protector, her champion, her confidant, and her lover. Oh, the past six months hadn't been without their share of tiffs and disagreements. It was hard going from being alone and making all her own decisions to having to consider someone else, especially someone as alpha as Zeke, but they were finding their way.

What helped was that Zeke had as much of a restless spirit as she did. The chalet was still their home base, but they'd taken several trips to various parts of the country. Traveling with Zeke was amazing. He didn't mind staying under the radar. In fact, he was quite good at it. And he was a boss at gathering information. Bonus—he gave the *best* back rubs… and other things.

She felt the heat rising in her face when she thought of what Zeke had given her just that morning. Nix's lips curled in a knowing smirk.

"I doubt kids are in our future," Aggie said honestly.

"No one says they have to be. The only thing that matters is that you do what's right for you. But, if you ever do decide to set up an east coast home base, Pine Ridge is a nice place to do it. You would fit right in."

Aggie couldn't agree more. The area was beautiful, a series of valleys nestled in the mountains. It held a lot of secrets, too. She knew only a little about the Callaghans and their Ghost Team, but it was enough to know that she and Zeke would be safe and in good company.

"Plus, you'd have me," Nix added.

A subtle pang of longing skittered through her chest. Aggie had never had a close friend. Her life—and her brother's—precluded such a thing. If the past six months had proven anything, however, it was that things Aggie thought she could never have now seemed possible.

"Thanks, Nix. I'd like that."

"I'll have Shane scout out some possible locations in the area for you."

"How many brothers are there again?"

"Seven. But the guys at Sanctuary are like family now too, and then there are the cousins over in Birch Falls."

Between the Callaghans and Sanctuary, Zeke would certainly have no shortage of former military guys to grab a beer with. Aggie said as much to

Nix.

"Yeah, bro time is as important as girl time. Speaking of, was Zeke excited about today?"

Zeke had confessed to her one night that he'd always wanted a classic Harley. That had planted the seed, and was one of the reasons she'd suggested they visit Pine Ridge after their last project. She told him she wanted to take a few days off and touch base with Nix, which was true, but she also wanted to surprise Zeke by getting him the motorcycle of his dreams. While Aggie and Nix had girl time, Sean had taken Zeke over into Birch Falls to meet with Kyle McCullough. Kyle was a cousin-in-law of the Callaghans and was legendary for his one-of-a-kind custom bikes.

"I didn't tell him. I wanted it to be a surprise. He thinks Sean's just keeping him out of our hair for a few hours."

Nix laughed. "Girl, that boy is going to rock your world tonight."

Aggie grinned widely. "Trust me, he does that every night. Why do you think I'm getting him the Harley?"

"Atta girl. I did something like that for Sean once. A former Army guy in Sumneyville opened up a garage there and specializes in restoring classic American muscle. I had him pick up a 1970 Dodge Super Bee, fix it up, and gave it to Sean for his birthday. He was so happy, I couldn't walk for a week."

"Here's hoping," Aggie said, raising her glass.

"Amen to that. And with luck, you'll get some good riding time in before *your good riding time*."

Aggie smiled, then grew serious.

"I'm going to tell him, Nix."

"You're sure?"

"Yes."

"Well, not that you need it, but you've got my blessing—and my promise that if he ever hurts you or abuses your trust, he'll never know what hit him."

EPILOGUE – PART II

~ *Zeke* ~

ZEKE APPRECIATED THE HEAVY, RUMBLING purr of the eight cylinders as Sean drove over the river from Pine Ridge to Birch Falls. The bridge was old, made of steel and cast iron during a different time.

Aggie was spending the afternoon with Nix, and he, apparently, was spending the afternoon with Sean. Zeke wasn't sure how he felt about that. He liked Sean, but it wasn't like they were buds or anything.

Sean shifted, the ink on his arm flexing with the movement. It was quality work, a Celtic symbol with a Da Vinci-like mechanical device done in incredible detail.

"Did you get that done around here?"

"Yeah, Tiny's over in Birch Falls. He does all the family ink."

"Does he take walk-ins?"

Sean glanced his way. "Why? You want to get something?"

Zeke nodded. He already had the design sketched out.

Sean grinned knowingly. "Robin, right? You're going to get her name tattooed over your heart or some shit like that."

"Maybe my ass."

Sean laughed. "You're all right, Zeke. We've got time. We can swing by and see if he can fit you in."

"You still haven't told me where we're going."

"All in good time."

Zeke snorted and looked out the window. He wasn't going to ask again. Since this trip didn't include a hypo to the neck, zip ties, and having his ass loaded and unloaded like a sack of potatoes, it was already a thousand times better than the last time he and Sean shared space.

"At least I'm conscious this time," Zeke mumbled, making Sean laugh.

They pulled up to the curb in front of a tattoo shop. It was small and didn't look like much from the outside.

"Don't judge a book by its cover," Sean said as if reading his mind.

Zeke didn't. Some of the best ink he'd ever gotten had been in places just like it.

"Hey, Sean," greeted a solid-looking woman with short black hair and an assortment of facial piercings. Every visible bit of skin below the neck was covered in intricate lacework ink.

"Hey, Kim," Sean replied.

"Are you finally going to let me give you that magic cross? I bet Nicki would love it."

Both men winced at the mention of the four-pronged penis piercing. "Not today, Kim. Not ever."

She laughed. "What can I do for you?"

"Zeke wants to get his woman's name tattooed on his ass."

Zeke sighed but didn't bother correcting him.

Kim looked Zeke up and down. "I think we can manage that. Tiny's just finishing up a client and doesn't have another one for a while. Go on and have a seat."

They did. Zeke picked up a design book and skimmed the pages. The guy's artwork was incredible. He should have no trouble doing what Zeke had in mind.

Before long, Tiny emerged from the back. Zeke's first thought: Tiny was anything but tiny. The guy was six and a half feet tall and had the build of a pro wrestler. Kim said a few words to him and pointed to where they sat.

Tiny greeted Sean and turned to Zeke. "Kim says you want your girl's name on your ass?"

Sean snickered.

"My chest, actually."

"Come on back, let's see what we've got."

* * *

Zeke and Sean left Tiny's less than an hour later. Tiny had done a phenomenal job of taking Zeke's ideas and working them seamlessly into the ink he already had.

"Where to now?" Zeke asked.

"Mo's."

"Who's Mo?"

"He runs a custom cycle shop. Robin said you like bikes."

He did, and looking at motorcycles was a nice way to kill time while Aggie was busy elsewhere.

Mo's cycle shop did not disappoint, especially when Sean led him around to the back and introduced him to Kyle McCullough. Kyle created legendary customs and specialized in old Harleys.

They talked about bikes and Kyle showed him some of the stuff he was working on. One bike in particular got his attention. It looked like the one he'd shown Aggie, only better.

"I just finished her," Kyle said. "Want to take her out for a ride?"

Zeke looked at him as if he'd lost his mind. "You're kidding, right?"

"I don't kid about bikes. Here." Kyle tossed him the keys. "Wheel her on out. Sean, you can use one of my spares. I'll get mine and we'll give her a road test."

Zeke looked at Sean in disbelief. Sean nodded. "I'd just go with it if I were you."

Zeke did. He pushed the bike out of the garage and climbed on. He gave it a powerful kick and the machine rumbled to life beneath him.

Kyle pulled up beside him and grinned. "Ready?"

Before Zeke could answer, Kyle took off like a bat out of hell.

Zeke was right behind him. For the next hour, Kyle led him them along winding mountain roads. The machine handled like a dream. When they returned to Birch Falls, Zeke was sorry the ride was over.

"That was fucking amazing," Zeke told him, clasping hands with Kyle. "Thanks, man."

"Glad you enjoyed it."

Zeke went to hand him back the keys, but Kyle just smiled. "Keep them. It's yours."

Zeke gaped at him. "Now I know you're fucking with me."

Sean appeared beside him. "No, he's not."

"How?" Zeke asked, but he knew. *Aggie.*

Sean smirked. "Feeling better about getting her name on your ass now, aren't you? The only question now is, can it make it back to the garage before my GTO?"

* * *

"You're fucking incredible, you know that?" Zeke said, pressing his lips to Aggie's neck as he slid into her again. Her skin was even more butter-soft than usual, smooth and radiant.

She tangled her hands in his hair and arched into him. "You like the bike."

"I love the bike. I can't believe you did that." No one had ever done anything like that for him. Ever.

"It wasn't completely selfless," she said huskily. "I never told you, but I've always had this secret biker fantasy, and you're exceeding my expectations again."

He raised and lowered his hips, setting a lazy rhythm. He could afford to take his time. He'd practically attacked her the moment she'd entered the hotel room and had spent the next several hours showing his appreciation.

This woman was everything. Everything he'd ever wanted. Everything he thought he could never have.

After he brought them both to their peaks, he rolled onto his back and pulled her close.

"I've been thinking."

"Uh-oh," he said softly.

"You were right."

"I usually am," he said without opening his eyes. "You'll have to be more specific."

"If we're going to be together, then you should know what you're signing up for."

"If? Sweetheart, I'm not going anywhere."

"You might not feel that way once you hear

what I have to say."

"Aggie, look at me."

She lifted her head and looked into his eyes. He waited until he had her full attention, then said, "Trust works both ways, and I trust that you'll tell me what I need to know when I need to know it."

"But what about—"

He stopped her words with a kiss. "This is all I need to know. Someday, if you're ready, you can tell me more."

"Yeah?"

"Yeah."

"In that case," she said working her way down his body, pausing to run her fingers lightly over his new ink, "I think it's about time I showed you my private island. And who knows? Maybe I'll even tell you my real name…"

Thanks for reading Zeke and Aggie's Story

You didn't have to pick this book, but you did. Thank you!
If you liked this story, then please consider posting a review online! It's really easy, only takes a few minutes, and makes a huge difference to independent authors who don't have the mega-budgets of the big-time publishers behind them.

Do you like free books? How about gift cards?

Sign up for my newsletter today! You'll not only get advance notice of new releases, sales, giveaways, contests, fun facts, and other great things each month, you'll also get a free book just for signing up ***and*** be automatically entered for a chance to win a gift card every month, simply for reading it!

Get started today! Go to **abbiezandersromance.com** and click on the **Subscribe** tab to sign up!

Also by Abbie Zanders

Contemporary Romance – Callaghan Brothers

Plan your visit to Pine Ridge, Pennsylvania and fall in love with the Callaghans

- Dangerous Secrets
- First and Only
- House Calls
- Seeking Vengeance
- Guardian Angel
- Beyond Affection
- Having Faith
- Bottom Line
- Forever Mine
- Two of a Kind
- Not Quite Broken

Contemporary Romance – Connelly Cousins

Drive across the river to Birch Falls and spend some time with the Connelly Cousins

- Celina
- Jamie
- Johnny

📖 Michael

Contemporary Romance – Covendale Series

If you like humor and snark in your romance, add a stop in Covendale

- 📖 Five Minute Man
- 📖 All Night Woman
- 📖 Seizing Mack

Contemporary Romance – Sanctuary

More small town romance with former military heroes you can't help but love

- 📖 Protecting Sam
- 📖 Best Laid Plans
- 📖 Shadow of Doubt
- 📖 Nick UnCaged
- 📖 Organically Yours
- 📖 Finding Home (Long Road Home / Sanctuary)
- 📖 Prodigal Son

More Contemporary Romance

- 📖 The Realist
- 📖 Celestial Desire
- 📖 Letting Go
- 📖 SEAL Out of Water (Silver SEALs)
- 📖 Rockstar Romeo (Cocky Hero Club)
- 📖 Cast in Shadow (Shadow SEALs)

Cerasino Family Novellas

Short, sweet romance to put a smile on your face

- 📖 Just For Me
- 📖 Just For Him
- 📖 Just For Her

Time Travel Romance

Travel between present day NYC and 15th century Scotland in these stand-alone but related titles

- 📖 Maiden in Manhattan
- 📖 Raising Hell in the Highlands

Paranormal Romance – Mythic Series

Welcome to Mythic, an idyllic communities all kinds of Extraordinaries call home.

- 📖 Faerie Godmother
- 📖 Fallen Angel
- 📖 The Oracle at Mythic
- 📖 Wolf Out of Water

More Paranormal Romance

- 📖 Vampire, Unaware
- 📖 Black Wolfe's Mate (written as Avelyn McCrae)
- 📖 Going Nowhere
- 📖 The Jewel
- 📖 Close Encounters of the Sexy Kind
- 📖 Rock Hard
- 📖 Immortal Dreams
- 📖 Rehabbing the Beast (written as Avelyn McCrae)
- 📖 More Than Mortal

Howls Romance

Classic romance with a furry twist

- 📖 Falling for the Werewolf
- 📖 A Very Beary Christmas
- 📖 Going Polar

Historical/Medieval Romance

📖 A Warrior's Heart (written as Avelyn McCrae)

About the Author

Abbie Zanders is the author of more than 55 published romance novels ranging from contemporary to paranormal and everything in between. She promises her readers two things: happily ever afters, always, and no cliffhangers, ever.

Born and raised in the mountains of Northeastern Pennsylvania, she has degrees in Computer Science and Mathematics. She worked for more than twenty-five years as a software engineer, designing and writing financial applications, though she has also held second jobs as a deli clerk, pub waitress, restaurant baker, and secretary that she draws upon to give real-life dimension to her characters.

Abbie has been crafting stories since elementary school, though she has only recently decided to start sharing them with others. When she's not escaping into another world of her own creation, she's a busy wife and mother of three, including a set of identical twins. Besides being an avid reader and writer, she loves animals (especially big dogs), American muscle cars, and 80's hair bands.

Made in the USA
Coppell, TX
09 March 2022

74729940R00155